Scribbles from the Sail Loft

AN ANTHOLOGY COMPILED BY
THE SAIL LOFT SCRIBBLERS

First printing: November 2012

ISBN: 978-0-9556215-3-6

Edited by Sonya Moore
Published by Angel Wings Publications
Cover design by Helen Weaver-Hills

Printed and bound by CPI Group (UK) Ltd, Croydon, CR0 4YY

Contents

Acknowledgements
About This Book

Acknowledgements

This book would not have been possible without the support of a great many people. We would like to express our thanks to the following: Pat Chesterton, Chairman of Combe Martin Museum, for all her practical help and enthusiasm; the volunteers who run Combe Martin Museum for their tolerance and good will; Mervyn Lethaby and his staff at The Royal Marine Public House and Hotel; Martyn and Jackie at the Galleon tea room, quizmaster Mike Bennett, the Arabic dance group Really Moorish and Kelly Beeston's ATS group Kalash for their fund-raising efforts; Ilfracombe Round Table, Ilfracombe Rotary Club and Combe Martin Parish Council for their generous donations; Judith Jones for her illustrations; Deborah McKinlay for her advice and guidance; Rosanna Rothery, Leisure Editor at the North Devon Journal for her support; Helen Weaver-Hills at Angel Wings Publications for her patience and hard work; and Helen Batstone for her invaluable editorial comments. We would also like to thank Petroc for starting us off on this journey and last, but in no way least, Sonya Moore, who has guided, cajoled and encouraged us to create this anthology.

The Sail Loft Scribblers
November 2012

About This Book

Sonya Moore

Petroc set us going like a fat gold watch. Two years ago, as a literacy lecturer, I taught a creative writing course at the Sail Loft in Combe Martin Museum. Now, retired, I continue to work with The Sail Loft Scribblers, a group of local people who share a joy in writing. This anthology is a collection of their work and these notes are an attempt to explain how they came into being.

"*All I Need Is Time*," wrote Berni, one of the Scribblers, in a parody of the Beatle's song, All You Need is Love.

Montessori developed an analogy of a circular clock to illustrate the amount of time it has taken for the earth to develop to its present state. Each hour represents 375 million years. We have been a species for one and a half million years, that's the last seven seconds of the clock!

Time is precious. It quickly disappears. This is why museums are so important as guardians of our heritage.

In the museum there is a book for sale: The Strawberry Fields, A Combe Martin Romance, written in 1952 by F V Follett. The language, style and content are so different to that of today.

Language reflects our culture, and The Strawberry Fields was written before most homes in Britain had television. Today, television, mobile phones and the internet take up half our waking life. Technology is driving language change and new interpretations of words. How do I know? I 'googled' it. A neologism is a newly coined term or word being widely used, but not yet accepted into mainstream language. Neologisms influenced *Intranet* and *Talking with the Kidz.* We made up our own words into nonsense poems like *Bargleflump.*

Follett, in the introduction to Strawberry Fields, says the poem "recalls older and slower modes of life... but the reader may be pleased to see something of them garnered before it's too late." Our lives, now, are very different, but the natural beauty of Combe Martin continues to inspire: *The Umber, Morning Walk, Combe Martin Bay.*

Our hobbies and interests are included as snapshots of our times: *It's Just Really Moorish, The Gift of Chocolate Ganache to Prince Harry, Small is More and Tiny is Even Greater.*

Marine Commando Knife and *Propeller* were influenced by artefacts on display in the Sail Loft. They are examples of concrete poems, the words following the contours of the topic.

Extracts from *Resolution* are scattered throughout the book. They are part of a collaborative story, inspired by photographs and information found in the museum. The story, entirely fictional, was set at the beginning of the last century. Different members of the group wrote parts of the story focusing on one character each.

There are guest appearances from writers from the Braunton Countryside Centre, whose mission is to increase the awareness of the coastal and farmed landscapes around Braunton.

This book is a child of our times, a celebration of local life; past and present. The work in it has been created through the hard work of the writers, support from friends, family and community.

It is a tribute to Combe Martin Museum, whose volunteers strive so hard to keep it open in these difficult financial times.

Our hope is that *"Scribbles from the Sail Loft"* will capture a moment in time, entertain and inform you, and, we hope, generate some income for the museum, so that all of us, now and in the future, can continue to enjoy our heritage.

On a Thursday we learn how to scribble

We drink tea and on biscuits we nibble

Metaphorically speaking

Our commas need tweaking

And our synonyms drip, leak and dribble

Strike Up Your Melodeon

So strike up your melodeon
And sing me Shammick tales
In the Sail Loft down on Cross Street
Where they used to store the sails

A green and fertile valley tumbles
Softly t'ward the rocky shore ·
Once Domesday peasants tilled their strips
And mutton grazed on open moor.
And later, village gardeners
Grew strawberries ripe and sweet for sale.
In taverns on the cobbled street
Old boys would yarn and sip their ale.
Evacuees found haven here
Safe from Hitler and his Blitz.
And Betsy Johnson, after school
Showed farmer boys her homework.

Sing me songs of silver lodes
Of minerals and miners
The clattering of donkey carts
Of ore for the refiners

Down in the harbour gently beached
With glistening catch the fishing boats
And lobstermen and crabbers too
Rowing out toward their floats
Maurice went lavering at low tide
Children played and children splashed
Where schoolgirls learned to swim like fish
Atlantic rollers sometimes crashed
Wreckers, aye! And smugglers too
Crept noiselessly upon the sand
At dead of night, without a light
And hid their chests of contraband

And bang those drums for the Irish Earl
Whose blood stained village hands
The 'Oss, the Fool, the Grenadiers
Who shot him on the sands

So strike up your melodeon
Where they used to store the sails
I love it when you sing to me
Those Shammick village tales

Bernadette Smoczynska

Two lads broke into the Wildlife Park
to steal a dinosaur, just for a lark,
but I'm pleased to say
they both ran away,
when a timber wolf howled in the dark.

The Earl of Rone

droning gets louder
drum beats announce their presence
hunting Earl of Rone

soldiers march along
pretty girls dance beside them
whimsical fool twirls

where is he hiding?
they march throughout the valley
children and adults

at last he is found
tethered backwards, blindfolded
for a donkey ride

led down the high street
onto the beach
hurled into rough waters

tumbled by waves
stoned by children
parents watch with glee

cheers rise and fall
as the sea swallows him
Earl gone forever . . .

again!

Helen Weaver-Hills

Morwenna's Plight

Olive Gallagher

Dusk was falling as the small cavalcade picked its way along the steep Devon hillside.

"We will not reach the village by nightfall," said the leading rider. "We would be better to make for the monastery and beg shelter for the night."

"No doubt you are right," replied the powerfully built man riding behind him. "But I shall have no delay – Morwenna shall be mine, by noon tomorrow or it will be ill for you."

Morwenna herself, guarded by a couple of Hugh of Barnstaple's henchmen, sat pale and miserable on her small pony. Tears still coursed down her cheeks as they had for many hours. Tomorrow she was to be given as a bride to the rich and despotic Sir Hugh, the most powerful man in the neighbourhood and older than her own father, John of Kentisbury. Morwenna cringed at the thought. She knew Sir Hugh was a man hated and feared by many and she could not bear the lascivious way his eyes roved over her slim young body. Her father was ambitious and thought the connection would increase his wealth and position. But what of Morwenna's feelings? She desperately loved young William of Kilpeck, who had journeyed into Devon from distant Herefordshire. Poor Morwenna felt she would rather die than marry Sir Hugh.

The group of riders reached the stout doors of the little monastery, and Sir Hugh knocked imperiously – cursing as they waited several minutes before the door was opened by a lay brother.

"The brothers are at vespers," they were told as they entered and Sir Hugh cursed again as his men tethered and baited the horses for the night. Father Augustine appeared eventually to enquire after the needs of his unbidden guests. He was a small and kindly man and his first thoughts were for the comfort of the distressed Morwenna. She was led to a tiny cell and given a meal of the simple fare that was provided for the monks. The men were given shelter for the night in the long common room.

Father Augustine heard the men discussing the impending marriage. He felt grave concern for the stricken looking girl. The visitors were provided with an ample supply of home brewed ale, and Father Augustine left them to spend the night in what comfort they could find. He slipped quietly away and visited Morwenna in her tiny cell. The kindly old man listened to her story, prayed with her and bade her not to despair.

Later that night, Father Augustine made his way down the rocky lane to the little village – a journey he had made so many times that it had no difficulties for him, even in the darkness. The church stood by the hillside, with a clear stream of water gushing from the twin springs under its foundations, even as it had in ancient times. He entered the church and stood before the altar in the dim light of the single oil lamp, then knelt down and prayed for guidance. He looked at the effigy of St Peter in his chains. There were many ways to be chained, he thought. Surely a forced and unhappy marriage would be one of them.

As he knelt, there was a slight commotion outside and he could hear the sound of horses being tethered as three young men entered the church. They stood with bowed heads until Father Augustine rose and addressed them, and then knelt themselves, before asking for his help. One introduced himself as William de Kilpeck – desperately seeking for Morwenna of Kentisbury and aided in his search by his good friends, Godfrey and Simon, from Hereford. Instructing the young men to wait where they were, the good Father retraced his steps to the monastery. He had a better chance to accomplish his errand alone than with noisy companions.

Just a few hours later in the quiet dawn light, Morwenna and young William de Kilpeck joined hands in marriage in St. Peter's Church. Her father and Sir Hugh of Barnstaple were still sleeping off the effects of the monastery home brew, but Morwenna felt no sense of guilt, only blessed relief and joy that was shared by her beloved William.

With all speed they left the silent building and rode down the narrow, rocky street, through the sleeping village towards the harbour. A boat was waiting and they boarded swiftly. Godfrey and Simon tethered the horses on deck. The boat slipped its moorings and made for the open sea across to Swansea, from where they would travel through Wales to reach Morwenna's new home in Herefordshire.

The young couple clung to each other in joy and relief. They turned for the last view of the village, with the sunlight just showing behind the conical hill – and their last glimpse of dear Father Augustine giving his blessing with a benign, numinous glow on his radiant face. He knew he had done the right thing.

meeting the master
quietly seeking answers
answer is silence

Combe Martin Bay

Should I never see Combe Martin bay again
Should I never see Combe Martin bay again
Should I watch no more the sun set from her shore
Then sad would my heart ever be

I have lived all my life in the cradle of this Combe
I have lived with the moor and the sea
I have lived, I have loved, and one day I shall die
In the only home ever meant for me

Should I never see...

If the cares of this world drive me sometimes from
your arms
How I long for the joy of return
As I gaze down the valley that leads unto your bay
My love for you never fails to burn

Should I never see...

Tell me what can compare Combe Martin to your vale
You're my friend, my lover and my wife
I might sail every sea and travel every road
But to live in you is all I ask of life

Should I never see...

Should I never see...

Ray Ashman

Resolution - Harry Cooke (1)

Olive Gallagher

The sun beat down mercilessly on the sweating troops as they boarded the train at Faisalabad. The men of the Devonshire Regiment had spent six gruelling days marching from Lahore Barracks over rough terrain to reach the nearest point to which the railway extended. How relieved they had been at the end of each day to pitch camp and enjoy a few hours respite. They were in a joyful mood.   It was the spring of 1910, and after a four and half year posting, they were on their way home to Devon.

Sergeant Harold Cooke, Harry to his friends, stood on the platform besides the crowded steam train, ensuring that the men of his unit boarded in an orderly manner, and that the native bearers loaded on the heavier equipment that had followed by oxcart.

At last, all was safely aboard; the bearers paid off and discharged. The regiment were on their way to Karachi, the waiting troop ship, and home at last to Devon.

After many stifling hours the train reached the port. Whilst transferring men, kit and property from train to ship, there was little time to indulge in thoughts of home. At last, all was safely stored; the men allocated their cramped sleeping quarters below decks, and all officers, NCOs and other ranks assembled on the deck of HMS *Shearwater*. The troops took their last glimpse of India to the sound of hearty cheers. Harry cheered as loudly as the rest, his handsome sunburnt face beaming with joy.

The engine throbbed as the ship left the harbour on the evening tide. The sun descended below the horizon. At last Harry had time to indulge in happy thoughts of returning home to his beloved family in

Combe Martin. How he longed to see his Mum again. She was a tiny lady, barely five foot tall, and still as pretty as a picture the last time he had seen her, with her dark curly hair and dark brown eyes. She was only forty now, merely sixteen when he was born.

Dad was much older, fair hair – just like his sister Lizzie and his two younger brothers. Harry wondered if his two brothers had grown much since he had last seen them. They were only lads of thirteen and fourteen when he had left for India. Now, they would be young men! Oh, they wouldn't believe some of the stories he had to tell and he would enjoy listening to the pranks they had been getting up to! Harry remembered them as little, wiry looking lads, but neither Mum nor Dad were tall. He grinned to himself at the recollection of being a head taller than his Dad on his eighteenth birthday – and now, he would be half as broad again at the shoulders! He stood on the darkened deck enjoying the cool night air and fresh sea breeze, thoughts still straying to home.

His Mum had told him that she met Dad when she went into service for the household of Sir Ralph Scrivener in Bideford. Mary was thirteen years old when she was first employed as kitchen maid and trainee cook. His Dad, Reuben, had already served the family for ten years as a gardener. Somehow, Dad had saved and scraped enough money together to buy three acres of arable land behind Granny Cooke's cottage in Combe Martin just before he married Mary and had started the prosperous market garden that supported the family.

Harry thought of the wonderful strawberries his Dad grew. He smiled – he'd be home just in time for the start of the season. He shook himself out of his reverie and descended to the lower deck. He checked that his men were assembled to file into the mess for a well deserved meal, and then joined his fellow sergeants for his own.

They spent a jolly evening together, but they were all exhausted by the events of the day. When, "Lights out!" was called they were glad to retire to their cramped quarters. Tomorrow would be a busy day with the customary lifeboat drill and some strenuous exercises for his men on the deck. Harry intended his men to be in tip-top condition and the smartest in the regiment as they marched through Barnstaple on their return to England.

Street Sounds

Soft whoosh of car passing through the night
Drunken louts spoiling for a fight
Twittering of birds as night gives way to light
Carnival costumes - wow! what a sight.

Chink of money hitting the ground,
Heavy breathing climbing the mound,
Blades whirling round high above the ground,
Wild animals scurrying without a sound.

Clip clop of horse trotting up the road,
Gentle croak of timid toad,
Rattle of mechanical load,
Zing of grass being mowed.

Plop, plop of rain in the puddle,
Young lovers entwined in clandestine cuddle,
Groups of people gathered in a huddle,
Jangle of sirens announcing trouble.

Helen Weaver-Hills

My Valentine

You are a tube of orange Smarties
A spicy dish of chilli prawns
A ruby red New World Shiraz
Served slightly warmed with vintage cheese
Coffee strong, hot, dark and sweet
Yes, I think you're all of these

Old Holborn in your baccy tin
The salty sea on sun warmed skin
We opened up the hives and breathed
The secret summer lives of bees
Honey, wax and woodsmoke curls
Of you I think when I smell these

Dum tak, dum dum tak, your drum beats out my
rhythm
On wintry nights you sing to me
And strum soft chords on your guitar
And then we stop ... and listen ... to the phatt bass
That shows us we're alive
And sends the blood around our veins
And Lady Gaga's Pokerface
Actually it's a lot quieter when you're asleep ...
Although not always

Like a pebble tumbled in the surf, somehow
You're smooth, but rough around the edges
Sometimes like a conker case you can be a little
prickly
Or like tippy toeing barefoot through a plate of frozen
peas
And yet, you're warm to snuggle up to
How can you feel like all of these?

Look at you! Look at you, with your swarthy skin
Those rock-pool eyes that twinkle from beneath yer
woolly 'at
By day some wild man from the hills with scruffy dog
And muddy boots and jeans all ragged at the knees
But ... at midnight ... you're my Arab prince
Ooh - be my Valentine, you tease!

Bernadette Smoczynska

bulbs darkly hiding
barren earth, awaiting spring
warmth brings new life

buds breaking open
leaves unfurl, flowers blossom
insects enjoy life

a beautiful boat
speeding over the water
seagulls flying by

magnificent scene
sand, waves, and sky meet the sea
stretching far away

night-time falls softly
moon rises in the sky
everything is quiet

Jack Norman (Nearer My God To Thee)

Jack Norman was raised a lime-burner's son
Which noble profession his father passed on
And being a man of perpetual good cheer
A God-fearing soul who knew right from wrong
As he tended the kiln Jack sang out this song
To ring down the valley for all folk to hear

Nearer my God to Thee
Nearer my God to Thee
Though I burn in lime
The Kingdom be mine
Nearer my God to Thee

Through springtime and summer by day and by night
Under Jack's supervision the kiln stayed alight
A gathering place the whole season long
Where quarrymen, burners and good farming folk
Shared cider and bacon, a yarn and a joke
And added their voices to Jack's rousing song

Nearer my God to Thee...

Then came a dark day when disaster befell
In most gruesome fashion the history-books tell
As he trod down the crust for the next load of stone
Jack slipped, overbalanced, then entered the fire
And yet as the lime burned him higher and higher
He sang out the tune he had made all his own

Nearer my God to Thee...

They pulled him alive from the quicklime and flame
Gave him spirits to drink to deaden the pain
Then sprawled in a handcart they trundled him home

Where sadly to tell he gave up the ghost
And died to the strains of his own sweet last post
As the lime-burners heralded Jack's kingdom come

Nearer my God to Thee...

Jack Norman's true story is one of the last
Of a once-great profession now lost to the past
But we who remember his like and his time
A kiln burning proud in a fine English field
And the workers who toiled to increase its yield
We salute you good Jack and all burners of lime

Nearer my God to Thee...

Ray Ashman

A young man went down to Wild Pear
to the beach, wearing nothing but air
he said "Gosh, I'm silly
it's really quite chilly."
but he sported his goosebumps with flair

Ernest Meets Nasty Sally Trench

Chris Batstone

Ernest and his new wife Marie were late again for breakfast in the little Combe Martin B&B. Conscious of the stares of the other guests who were already seated and eating, the couple tried to surreptitiously creep to their table. Unfortunately, Ernest could not stifle a large yawn and Marie added to his embarrassment by announcing loudly to their landlady that she was so hungry that morning that she could eat a horse. However his good mood was soon restored by sweet, freshly smoked kippers and creamy Devon butter on toast.

After breakfast, they strolled up the high street, pausing to investigate the various novelty goods on sale in the shops. They admired sea shells laid out in wickerwork baskets, the pink and gold of mother-of-pearl shimmering in the morning sun. With the new shared intimacy that comes to newlyweds, the couple took a particular interest in some rather risqué postcards on display. After much deliberation, they purchased two cards. One, a drawing of a young girl with a bull which had them in fits of giggles; the other of a more sober watercolour view of the harbour, suitable to send to her parents. Satisfied with their purchases, they walked on to the beach.

It was the second day of their honeymoon. Ernest was beginning to get into the spirit of a seaside holiday. Today he wore his shirt with the collar open and was sporting a snazzy, striped blazer and a boater, with a hatband in the colours of their athletic club. Marie had a rather daring cotton dress and was determined to catch as much sun as was decently possible. By the time they reached the beach it was already quite crowded. A young lad with unkempt red hair and an upturned nose offered them deck-chairs. With great deliberation, he carefully put their coins into the pocket on the front of his calico apron and fetched two folded chairs for them.

"Where would 'ee like to sit, sir?" he asked.

"We don't really mind, thank you," Ernest replied, unfamiliar with the beach.

"In the sun, please," added Marie, hopefully.

The boy found them a gap among the other sunbathers, facing the sun but in the lee of a rocky promontory. "This idn a bad place to be, gets the sun in the middle o' the day and you'm owt o' the breeze," he said, to Ernest's delight.

With a flourish, he opened the wooden and canvas deck-chairs and settled them onto the shingle. Ernest held the chair for Marie to sit, then removed his blazer before making himself comfortable. He could see Marie out of the corner of his eye. Having checked that no-one was watching, she let her body slump into the chair, causing her dress to ride up to her knees. He loved the way she made him feel so alive. Conscious of his gaze, she reached over and squeezed his hand.

"Love you," she said.

"And I love you too." Ernest felt like the luckiest man on earth.

Soon, the heat of the sun and the gentle washing of the waves on the beach lulled them into a gentle doze.

"You! Yes, you two!" A sharp female voice shattered their tranquillity. "You must move at once. That is my place!"

A rather striking woman - handsome rather than beautiful - with long, crow-black hair was marching towards them. Ernest jumped to his feet, knocking the deck-chair which collapsed flat onto the shingle. Flustered, he blurted out, "My deepest apologies, madam, the young deck-chair attendant put us here."

"Him? He's a fool. I taught him for seven years and he learnt nothing." She planted herself in front of the couple, fixing Ernest with a cold stare. She held a battered black Gladstone bag in one hand, and was brandishing a plain black umbrella in the other. "Well come on, then. I haven't got all day. Out of my place."

"Um – You have me at a disadvantage. I don't quite see how this can be your place, ah, Madam," said Ernest, made a little braver by his desire to protect Marie's happiness. "There are other spaces."

"Tch! They won't do at all. I can tell that you are not a local, boy, and by the look of you I don't suppose that you paid much attention at school." Ernest opened his mouth to speak, then closed it again. His mind had gone blank.

"I thought not," she said. She turned towards Marie. "I suggest you cover yourself up too. This is a public beach in Combe Martin, not some backstreet in Buenos Aires!"

Marie blushed, and frantically tugged at the hem of her dress. The woman took another step towards Ernest. "Well come on! I can feel my face burning! If the ozonious gases make my skin turn, it will be your fault!"

"Gas? Burn your face?" Ernest was reeling under the onslaught.

"Of course! I have a very fragile complexion, being from an old English family with fair skin, with no foreign blood that can tolerate the sun." She shot a furious glance at Marie.

That was it. Ernest steeled his resolve. He picked up his deck-chair and held it defensively in front of himself. A sudden understanding had dawned on him. He wondered, could this lady possibly be behaving just like any other vain female customer worried about her appearance? Was she hiding her embarrassment by being short with the staff? His finest flattery and charm were needed.

"Of course, Madam. I can see that you have a most delicate complexion. If I may be so bold, I would think you to be just a young girl had you not mentioned your years spent labouring in the classroom."

The woman pursed her lips and breathed out slowly.

"Yes well ..." Ernest continued, "Let me introduce myself. I am Ernest Potts of Potts Emporium. We stock only the very finest salves and creams for our most exclusive clientele. May I ask, have you tried Mrs. Minerva-Trumpton's Patent Resilience Face Cream? Formulated exclusively for the Estonian Royal Family, and, I have it on good authority from my supplier that it is delivered to the London home of Princess Georgiana!"

She sniffed dismissively. "Propriety and financial probity are my watchwords."

"But Madam, such a fair skin deserves nothing but the best. I quite assumed that you must have been using it regularly." As he said this, Ernest carefully put down his chair. He could see her hesitate and pressed home his advantage. "I have a suggestion. May I introduce Marie, my wife? Marie, did you pack any of Mrs. Minerva-Trumpton's Patent Resilience Face Cream?"

Taking his hint, Marie delved into the large canvas bag that she had packed for the beach.

"Yes, darling," she replied, holding a small glass jar with an elaborate emerald green and gold label. "I have a new pot here."

The woman's gaze shifted to the ornate jar.

"May I offer this to you?" asked Ernest. "Thinking now, I don't believe that it is available anywhere in the West Country." The woman's face slowly cracked into a smile.

"For me? I couldn't. But... Yes, yes please. Not available anywhere in the West Country you say?"

"Madam..."

"Sally Trench, please."

"Miss Trench, let me assure you that Potts is one of only a very few stockists of this extraordinary preparation in the country." Ernest took the jar and proffered it to her. "If you find it to be suitable for you, Potts Emporium would be delighted to supply you on a regular basis."

"Well, I might give it a try." Her hands closed around the jar and, with some alacrity, she turned to go. "Ah... Thank you. Oh, and if I want more, how will I contact you?"

Ernest smiled. "I think that we will be right here on the beach for the next few days."

On his new bike rode young Joe Munder
along Wild Pear cliff in the thunder
fell straight down to the sands
as he shouted "No hands!"
no control and no skill, so no wonder.

Milking Time

Cows gently amble up the track way,
quiet hoof-fall, tails swish flies away.
Warm bovine smells fill the early air,
fresh cudded grass on breath, hide and hair.
Morning birdsong chirrups from hedgerow,
blackbird, dunnock, chaffinch and sparrow.
Spring grass dung plops, splashes on concrete,
gates clang shut; tight uddered matrons wait.
Switch on vacuum pump, droning hum noise,
pulsators beat out ka-boosh, ka-boosh.
Rattle feed into plastic wall troughs,
eager cows surge in to crunch the nuts.
Standing in a row, ready to milk,
wipe teats clean, fragile skin soft as silk.
Put on milking cups, gentle suction,
watch milk flow, admire cows' production!
Take off cluster, as each cow completes,
Rub on emollient to relaxed teats.
Another clang crash, from five rail maze,
happy mooing as then out to graze.

Chris Batstone

The Umber

From your source high on the hill
You come rushing downward still
Playing like a little child
Ever running, wet and wild.
Dashing, flashing, splashing down
Hurrying to reach the town.
On your ancient rocky bed
Countless ages you have sped
Shouting, laughing gleefully
In your haste to reach the sea

Foaming, swishing down the hills
Splashing reeds and daffodils,
Gurgling, bubbling all the way
Never for a moment stay.
Joined by the cascade by the church
You rush onwards in your search
Passing parks and gardens gay
You flow onwards night and day
Off to meet your destiny
In the wild and raging sea.

Curving, swerving, in a dream
You meet with the Rosea stream
Then go plunging out of sight
Never stopping in your flight.
Reappearing at the beach,
Now the sea's within your reach
You can't wait to meet the tide,
Like a young and wilful bride.
Leaping, laughing, joyously
Rushing down to meet the sea.

Streaming wildly down the sand
Your ripples make a sparkling band
With a foaming frothy trail
Like a lovely lacy veil.
You pour at last into the sea
Together for eternity.
The Umber still flows down the hill.
Always has and always will
Ever running, constantly
From its source into the sea

Olive Gallagher

Now, Jane was a cute little number
though out on her bike she might slumber
on a hill very steep
she once went to sleep
and fell flat on her face in the Umber.

The Wrong Side of the Pond

The lament of a small pond creature after being on the receiving end of a session of Pond Dipping by a class of enthusiastic nine year olds.

I've had a really dreadful day,
the worst one of the year!
I'm still a heap of misery
and eaten up with fear.
Forgive me if I bore you,
but wouldn't you complain
If you'd been dragged out of your pond
and thrown back in again.
Not once. Or twice. But twenty times!
(It seems like even more!)
My nerves are shot to pieces and
I'm very bruised and sore.

They caught me in a fishing net
and dropped me in a pail
Along with several tadpoles
and some beetles and a snail.
I found a piece of water weed
and tried to hide behind it
So they put me in a smaller pot
and thought I wouldn't mind.
I jumped about in terror
while my stomach churned inside me
As they slowly turned the airtight lid
and greatly magnified me.

They thought I was a Water Nymph,
a Boater or a Skater!
(The teacher wasn't very sure
and said she'd find out later)
They thought I was a Caddis Fly
and counted all my legs
They looked me up in worksheets
to find out if I laid eggs
They studied all my segments
and inspected every gill
And they tried to draw my feelers
but I wouldn't keep them still.

At last I'm safely home again
and back with all my friends,
I've warned them to be careful
or they'll come to sticky ends.
And as for me I'll keep well down
and really get my skids on
To keep away from noisy kids
and little pots with lids on.
For even though I've lost a leg
and swim with quite a limp
I am NOT a Water Boatman.
I'm a proper Water Shrimp!

June Cragg

Resolution - Lily

Helen Weaver-Hills

Lahore? 'Where's that?' Lily wondered. She'd never heard of it. Had she? Is it somewhere she should know? She wanted desperately to ask her friend Maisie, who sat next to her, but it was forbidden to talk in class. So she didn't dare. Last time she did that Maisie was punished as well and it wasn't her fault. But oh, she so wished she could speak to her. Maisie seemed to know everything - or so it felt to Lily.

" . . . so there we were, the cannon all lined up, the soldiers waiting for orders to come from Lahore HQ . . ." the soldier went on.

Reluctantly she turned her attention back to what was being said. There was nothing for it. Lily just had to know *where* they were talking about so, after pausing for a brief second, up shot her arm - before she could change her mind. The soldier paused. He looked straight at Lily and said "Something you want to ask?"

"I . . . um, well . . . I don't know where Lor is," she said, in little more than a whisper. Everyone was looking at her. She felt so silly but no one had explained - or had she been day-dreaming instead of listening at the crucial moment?

There was a deathly silence.

Then the thunderous voice of Mr. Stokes bellowed across the classroom. Lily shrank down into her seat. It was always her - why didn't the others ever ask questions? Or ever say anything for that matter. She felt the tears form in her eyes. It wouldn't do to cry - it only made him worse than ever. He hated her. She was sure of it. But why? What had she ever done except to try her best to do what was expected of her. To learn. The very reason she was at school, to learn.

For some unfathomable reason her attempts to acquire knowledge were not heeded or appreciated.

"Come out here, girl!"

With head bowed down, trying not to weep, Lily stood up slowly. The soldier looked kindly at her but didn't dare intervene, though he was puzzled by the teacher's reaction. The little girl was right. He should have had a map so that the children could see for themselves exactly what part of the world he was talking about. He mentally chastised himself and vowed to do better another time, though whether it would ever be here, in the village school, was another matter.

Lily took several tentative steps towards Mr. Stokes and as she did so, she noticed a suggestion of a smile on the soldier's lips. She immediately turned her face away but she'd seen enough to know that he, at least, didn't mind the question. It gave her fresh courage - at least someone was on her side. She had no idea how all the other children sitting behind her felt, but here was a grown-up who didn't mind that she had spoken up.

She momentarily lifted her face to look straight at Mr. Stokes, who instantly exploded, red-faced, with his eyes almost popping out of his head.

"How dare you defy me! Put out your hand . . ."

Thwack! Thwack! went the ruler. Lily flinched twice as she tried to pull her arm from his iron grip. The tears were coursing down her face now and as soon as he let go she flew out of the classroom as fast as her legs could carry her . . . she was breathless and sobbing as she ran down the road until she reached the harbour. She could see her father's boat moored alongside the jetty.

"Daddy! Daddy!" She almost slipped as she charged down the broken steps where, safe at last, she fell into her father's arms.

Colours of the Sea

So green the hills beneath the morning sky
So sweet the breeze filled with loud seagulls cry.
There on the cliffs the purple heather clings
Whilst high above the little skylark sings
And then dives swiftly by the streamlet's course
To reach her nest amongst the golden gorse.

Below me, wavelets ripple on the beach
And on the distant rocks beyond my reach
The clamouring seagulls gather to explore
The seaweed debris strewn along the shore.
A cormorant dives, then rises yards away –
The curlew wades to search along the bay.

Below me now, the ocean's wide expanse
Where tiny waves with gold and silver dance
The foam along the rocks reflects the light
Of tiny droplets shining diamond bright
While pools of amethyst, aquamarine
And shining jade complete the view serene.

Olive Gallagher

Dad

Dad with mouth open
Lying exhausted in bed
Infection rampant.

Antibiotics
Struggling with the invasion
Retrieving control.

Struggling to swallow
To absorb nutritious food
Takes ages to eat.

Life slipping away
Breathing slows down, eating stops
No energy left.

Is it bye, bye Dad?
After ninety-five long years
Leaving us behind . . .

. . .

Not a bit of it.
Two weeks later he is up
He is dressed

He is eating
He is well
He's done it again!

Helen Weaver-Hills

On Choosing a New Tribal Skirt

Twenty five yards each of frill and of flounce
A multicolour vibrant siren song
Languidly hanging yet ready to pounce
One could lose one's heart if one were not strong.
Frothy cascades of deep green forest glades
Wide summer skies and the swirls of the sea
Hot fiery earth flows, a riot of shades
Shivering daffodils - all scream "Pick Me!"
But what if I chance to choose the wrong one?
Like puppies not picked they'll stay with the rest
As ghosts in my head 'til end of the sun.
Black is my friend, maybe black would be best.
Then as I ponder on what I should do
      The Tarot reveals I have to buy two!

Bernadette Smoczynska

My Street

Don Hills

I live in King Street, formerly known as Queen Street in the reign of Queen Victoria. It's part of a long, straggling road, which effectively embraces five streets. It's just a little bit up from the harbour in Combe Martin, and many of the fisher folk used to live here. In its time it has seen a great variety of shops – for example only just opposite, there used to be a bank and a baker's shop. The bank has gone now, but the baker's survives – a bit of a miracle really, as there's a grocer's shop selling bread, cakes etc just two doors from our house, with the ever-present hypermarket only a few miles away on the outskirts of Ilfracombe. Digging a little deeper into the history of the street has revealed a fascinating combination of circumstances affecting the lives of my predecessors.

It became clear, for example, that many of the residents must have been searching for employment other than the fickle fishing industry. Those with sailing skills would have sought to trade across the Bristol Channel, exporting local agricultural produce such as strawberries and importing coal to fuel the machines used in extracting mineral ores such as silver-lead. It takes quite a stretch of the imagination to envisage the varied life of neighbours along King Street – miners living next door to agricultural labourers, fishermen rubbing shoulders with traders of all kinds.

The coming of the Turnpike Roads (from 1866 in the case of Borough Road next to King Street) was as influential in the effective movement of goods and services as the use of boats. There is no doubt that my predecessors needed to be highly resourceful in not merely eking out a living, but in actually creating conditions for relative prosperity. A good example is those who took advantage of the development of tourism in the late nineteenth century. Some would have used their fishing boats for taking visitors around the Bay. Others would have let out rooms for bed and breakfast. Many, I'm sure, would have been in the thick of organising and taking part in the Village Carnival. Living in the community, I get the taste of this each year as the excited participants process past my house, bands playing and colours flying.

What incredible changes, then, my street has seen through the years. Now many, perhaps most residents are 'incomers', with a fair proportion of these being, like me, retired. Some things though, seem to have changed little. It's still a very noisy place, with lorries arriving during the night to stock up at the grocer's, and enthusiastic, lively young people, who cachinnate as they enter and exit the club rooms opposite my house.

Another unchanging feature is the incredible view of the high hills as you lift your eyes above the houses on either side of the road. In springtime, the sheep with their lambs still move contentedly along the skyline munching the delicious grass.

In many ways we have the best of both worlds – the rural and the marine. Gone are the heavy machines of an earlier age pumping out their fumes, which caused some observers to describe Combe Martin as a kind of Dickensian, smoke-filled industrial village. In its place my street retains something I have always wanted: a place where the land meets the sea in a satisfying embrace.

In a pub down beside the sea wall
we saw Uncle Tom Cobley and all
they'd come on a horse
it was wooden of course
and about twenty-seven feet tall.

Time Is All I Need

Time – Time - Time
There's so much I'd do if I had the time
Jumpers to knit that are waiting in line
Dances to dance, cakes I need to bake or if I ever had
the chance
Walk the coast path

There's TV shows waiting for me on the hard drive
Books pile up patiently in the hall
I will learn to play the piano one day
And walk the coast path

All I need is time. All I need is time
Just a bit more time – Please - Time is all I need
Time - Time - Time
All I need is time - All I need is time
Just a bit more time – Please - Time is all I need

There's so many places that I'd like to see
Plenty of places I'd just like to be
Rivers to kayak and hills that I'd like to climb
Along the coast path

All I need is time - All I need is time
Just give me more time - Time - Time is all I need
All I need is time (I'd really like to retire)
Just a bit more time (with all the time I desire)
All I need is time - Time - Time is all I need

Berni Smoczynska

Small is More and Tiny is Even Greater

Helen Weaver-Hills

A magnifying lens is held in place by a band round my head. A bright light shines behind a tiny piece of ivorine, about two by three inches, mounted onto a light box in readiness for me to begin the delicate process of creation. The brush is one of the smallest you can buy; so small I cannot see the actual tip of the bristles. Ivorine is a synthetic version of ivory and the most commonly used surface for miniature paintings. It is translucent and has been de-greased immediately prior to starting to paint, by using a little talc. It has also had a faint wash applied to give a background to the painting I am about to start. I can see my design, previously drawn on paper and placed underneath, showing through the almost translucent quality of the ivorine. The lines provide a guide as to where I should place each dot of paint, enabling me to bring the design to life, using techniques crucial to the creation of a miniature painting.

With a sense of trepidation, I dip my brush into clean water and wipe off the excess on a piece of kitchen towel. Previously chosen colours have already been prepared on a palette and left to dry. With the tip of the brush, I pick up a tiny amount of the first colour I am going to use, test it out on the edge of the ivorine and, if all is well, take a deep breath and make the first dot in the appropriate position. With steadfast concentration, ensuring it is just the very tip of the brush that touches the ivorine, I place more dots close together but not touching, allowing other dots (of possibly different colours) to be placed in between once the original dots are dry. In this way I can create the illusion of a third colour, which results from the eye being tricked by the juxtaposition of the first two.

I continue in this fashion until . . . *Drat!* My mind had wandered for an instant, allowing the brush to deposit too much paint, creating an over-sized dot. It has to be removed. I select another brush – dry, this time – and carefully place it in the centre of the rogue dot, drawing up the excess paint. I repeat the treatment and leave it to dry off completely.

Oh, well! There are plenty more areas needing my attention, so I start over in a different part of the picture. This time it is a major part of the background, which needs to be covered using a more efficient method. Using a similar process, this time I draw extremely fine, short lines. Like the dots, I have to take care to keep the lines from touching each other. I make some headway. The painting is beginning to take shape, though I am a long way from completion.

After a significant break, the earlier abandoned section is now dry and I can return to using pointillism on the previously repaired area. Slowly the painting is being built up layer by layer, area by area, until the desired effect has been achieved.

Constructing a miniature painting requires a steady hand, focused concentration and endless patience. Although it is possible to use other media, such as acrylics and oils, the joy of working with watercolours on ivorine is the ease with which one can erase one's errors and start again!

Mistakes notwithstanding, the delight I feel as I behold my design slowly coming to life is magical. My mind is focused. My body is relaxed, for tension does not help the composition. Leaving the work-table to release muscle tension and change the focus of the eyes is essential but never welcome, unlike long stretches of uninterrupted time.

Hours, days and sometimes weeks later the picture is eventually finished, polished, sealed and ready to be placed in a complementary frame, behind specially produced fine glass to protect the precious work.

–◆–

five people sitting
studious looks on faces
silence reigns throughout

invigilator
sternly silent and alert
watching over all

A Saucy Seaside Saga

Young Albert went down to North Devon,
with his beautiful, blushing new bride,
for a honeymoon in Combe Martin,
two weeks by the sunny seaside.

They were staying in a little hotel,
on the road below Hangman path.
The room had a small bed with chintz covers,
but an en suite with a very large bath.

"That bed is too small for us both,"
said Albert with a glint in his eye.
"But if thee's in the mood to be rude,
we could give the bath a good try!"

Now young Albert believed in self improvement,
and was keen to learn whenever he could.
On seeing a notice about a big exhibition,
thought the experience would do them both
good.

He enquired of the local bus service,
found an omnibus that went all the way,
bought two tickets without hesitation;
they were in Barnstaple by mid-day.

It was the Jubilee celebration,
for Queen Victoria, long on the throne.
Exhibits from all of the Empire,
a carnival second to none.

Pride of place was an Indian tankard,
a replica of one sent to the Queen,
with figures from the Karma Sutra,
doing things that were quite obscene.

The couple stared transfixed. She asked,
"Is it me or is it hot in here?"
"By heck! You're right, I'm getting quite sweaty.
Let's go out for a breath of fresh air."

Said Albert, "them foreign fellows is nowt but
disgusting,
it must be the heat or the food!"
But the images had got them both thinking
of activities decidedly lewd.

But his bride was a practical lass,
she wanted a cream tea first,
and by the time they'd ate all the strawberries,
they felt as if they just might burst.

By evening, Albert was getting impatient,
keen to cuddle his lovely young bride.
So early to bed for the couple,
as his enthusiasm had got hard to hide.

With much giggling and creaking of bedsprings,
they passed the honeymoon night away,
but surprised all the other residents,
by going back into town the next day.

The other guests were most impressed,
that they went back to the exhibitions.
But it wasn't to study the British Empire,
but to learn new bedroom positions.

I thank you!

Chris Batstone

Resolution - Harry Cooke (2)

Olive Gallagher

The sun had risen early on a beautiful June morning, although its golden rays had taken some time to send their long fingers over the hill to the sheltered slopes above Combe Martin village. Already the entire Cooke family were busy picking the luscious crop from their prize strawberry beds. The early dew was dry on the fruit so there was no chance of mould forming on the berries before the consignment reached the London markets.

Harry stood upright for a minute, rubbing his aching back. It was the first time for many years that he had joined his family in this occupation. Although he was no stranger to hard work, his back muscles were beginning to complain. He looked with pleasure at his busy siblings, nimble fingers snipping off the stems at just the requisite length at such a speed. They kept companionably close , each having started on a different row, so they kept within a yard of each other as the morning progressed. His brothers, Phil and Bob, kept up a lively banter, occasionally teasing Lizzie, although she only laughed at them in return.

As he gazed over the beautiful valley Harry realised how much he had missed his home in the long years he had spent in India. He had seen so many wild and exotic places, strange cities, remote villages, jungles and mountain ranges, but he felt there was nothing to compare with the scenery before his eyes at this very moment. The varied greens of the surrounding hillsides, the lower slopes dotted with little farms and market gardens like their own; all breathed tranquillity.

On the upper slopes flocks of sheep were grazing, slowly ambling around the darker groups of gorse bushes that dotted the hillside. He looked across the narrow valley to the grazing cattle in the high meadows beyond, and the woodlands filled with chestnut, larch, ash and willow. Down below him was the long winding village street. He could just make out the top of the church tower. Ahead of him the steep hillside sloped down to the beach and busy little harbour with its fantastic array or rocks and cliffs. The sea was alive and dancing in the sunlight, grey, jade green and as many blues as one would find on an artist's palette. To his right he could see the top of the pyramid shape of Little Hangman Hill and his eyes followed the more gradual incline to Great Hangman. Somebody had once told him it was the highest sea cliff in the whole of England. He could well believe it!

Harry bent once more to his task. He appreciated how much hard work his family had put into their few acres of land under his Dad's supervision. The land was good and almost lime free as strawberries do not thrive with lime. Plenty of good manure was dug into the soil and new plants were grown in rotation. Three or four years were the maximum time for strawberry plants to be their most productive. Many gruelling hours were spent in weeding and layering underneath the plants with barley straw.

He listened to the songs of the blackbirds and thrushes. Sometimes the birds were a nuisance as they also liked to eat the ripe fruit – but in compensation they also devoured the slugs, snails and insects which caused more damage.

Now it was mid-morning and Mum arrived from their cottage below with the large enamel jug and mugs so they could all enjoy a well-deserved drink of tea as they had all worked up a tremendous thirst.

Reuben looked with affection at his wife. In their twenty five years of married life he had never had one regret and was always happy in the harmony of their home and family. He was proud of Harry too.

The Rock

White horses charging at its feet
The salt-splattered rock stands firm,
Looking out across the wind-swept bay,
Wondering how all the undersea creatures
Thrive in such turbulent conditions
Throwing up driftwood left to decompose nonchalantly.

Musing on bygone times as the stream tumbles down
the hillside
Joining the calisthenics of moon-driven waters;
As did the Normans when they arrived in Combe
Martin
Where many industrial activities thrived -
Mining, quarrying and strawberry-growing.

Listening to voices hollering through the fertile valley;
The clatter of hooves and clang of metal
As engines grind along narrow rails,
Sighs of workers when cholera strikes the note of
doom
And lays the people low, disrupting the very fabric of
village life.

Helen Weaver-Hills

Marine Commando Knife

The
Knife
sharp
slashes
slices
slivers
severs
soldiers
stabs
slits
cuts
guts
spill
kills
you
me
I

Chris Batstone

It's Just Really Moorish

Bernadette Smoczynska

Autumn, 1995. Timidly stepping into my first belly-dance lesson, I had no idea that I was stepping through the doorway to a whole new world. A world of hauntingly beautiful music and insistent rhythms, a world where I would learn about the culture and history of a people, a world of colour, sparkles and sequins where my penchant for dancing without shoes is the norm. I have made many new friends and been privileged to learn from teachers from all over the world. These days I prefer to call it Arabic dance because I feel it better reflects what I do. The word "belly-dance" conjures up all kinds of salacious images and I'm sorry, guys, but I'm just not that kinda gal.

The origins of this dance are lost in the mists of time. Some consider that it evolved from the ritual dances of our ancestors, from the focus in ancient worlds on fertility, regeneration and the mystery surrounding the continuation of life. There is no doubt that the dance moves strengthen and tone all the relevant muscles in that respect. In the Arabic world this dance is an art and a skill, a legacy passed down through the generations from mother to daughter.

One theory is that the term belly-dance is a corruption of the Arabic word *baladi* meaning "of the country" or "of the people", so it's the dance of the people of the Arabic countries. All the people do it. Men and women, the young and the maybe not so young, people of all shapes and sizes, albeit within cultural boundaries. And in the same way as language is enriched by dialect, so the Middle East has a plethora of dance styles as well as costume styles.

Over the years I have dipped and dabbled and thoroughly enjoyed. The Khaleegy dance is fun, for example. Bedouin in the desert originally danced this dance, wearing diaphanous, jewel encrusted *thobes* over their everyday clothing. The moves and gestures used in this follow-the-leader party dance signify good wishes and prosperity and it is still enjoyed today by the ladies of the Arabian Gulf. These days, however, they are more likely to be wearing designer clothing under their *thobes*.   In complete contrast there is Rai, the subversive blues of Algeria. There are the energetic, traditional scarf dances of North Africa and the Guedra trance dance of the Touareg.   And let's not forget those naughty Persian ladies and their irreverent, tongue in cheek send up of their macho men in the Baba Karam.

Yes, it's been fun, but always I find that I am drawn back to all things Egyptian. I feel comfortable dressed in voluminous harem pants, *galabeya* and coined hip-scarf and with my head swathed in scarves and veils, there is no need to worry about bad hair days.   My alter ego, Fatima, has no need of a purse because her wealth is sewn onto her clothing or worn on her ears, neck, wrists and ankles so that she jingles as she moves.   She is an earthy, grounded, barefoot Saaidi queen.   Her body is unable to resist the simple timeless rhythms of the Nile.   The dum tak of the *tabla* is her heartbeat, while the accordion and wailing *mizmar* transport her to ancient places. She loves to entertain at local *haflas* with her flat footed hip-drops and Egyptian walk, a shimmy of the shoulders and a twinkle in her eye.

In the present, yet rooted deeply in the past we share our shimmies, swings and sways with our maternal ancestors, our hips tracing the circles and loops of infinity, without beginning and without end across the face of time.

Boardroom Battle

An excerpt from a notional '70's style' blockbuster...

Chris Batstone

Previously...The hero, Dave Collard, financial director, supported by the other directors, is in a battle for control of his company with the charismatic, ambitious chairman Sir Stephen Bradley. Together, they founded the original business but now the chairman wants to take the company in a direction that will benefit his career but not the company in the long term. The directors, who have been happy to let Sir Stephen have all the limelight, now have to find a way to appeal to the shareholders at an emergency general meeting. The chairman enjoys the support of a large pension fund that has a substantial share holding in the company and which the smaller shareholders have tended to follow in the past. It is late afternoon. The directors have had their last meeting with the chairman to try to dissuade him before the EGM. It has not gone well. The chairman is confident that he will win. Dave is back in his office. *Now read on...*

I tried swearing; I put together all the worst words that I could muster and used them to curse the chairman. It didn't help dispel the churning in my stomach. I felt cross, frustrated and, to be honest, frightened.

I checked my emails; nothing that wouldn't keep until tomorrow, then rang my secretary.

"Margaret. I'm going home. I think I need to let off steam in the gym."

"That's fine Mr. Collard, see you tomorrow."

"Thanks Margaret."

I was already taking off my tie as I strode through security. I felt better being outside and walked quickly to the gym, only a few hundred yards from our main entrance.

It was worth going that little bit earlier. The members who trained in the evening were yet to arrive. Spoilt for choice of apparatus, I started on the treadmill, choosing a medium running pace but at a steep incline. Soon I was panting and I eased back the incline, happy to let my legs move at their own volition while my mind went over the events of the day. The big flat screen TVs in the gym were blasting out dance music and I let the sound envelop me. After twenty minutes I switched to the rowing machine and tried to beat my personal best for two thousand meters. It was a good time but not a record. I tried some shoulder presses but I had burnt off my adrenalin and my thoughts were back with the forthcoming EGM. I would shower, go home, eat and have an early night; things might seem clearer in the morning.

My route home from the gym took me past the public library; its large art deco facade dominating the line of small shops to either side of it. I went in, not knowing what I was looking for, and drifted around the shelves of reference books. It seemed to smell of quiet; wood polish, old paper and dust against a background of muffled conversations and the odd squeak of a rubber sole on the floor. Self improvement, accounting, computing - some books there that should be in a museum - marketing and management guides. With a growing sense of futility I concluded that there would be no easy answer here and turned to go.

A tiny book caught my eye. Its cover was faded and torn; the laminate peeling off. The Art of War by Sun Tzu. I knew that it was a classic set text for many military and management training courses. I opened it at random and started reading. I ignored the commentary and dived straight into the simple lines of prose translated from the ancient Chinese. A discreet gong sounded announcing that the library would be closing in five minutes. I checked out the little book and hurried home.

Once indoors, I kicked off my shoes, slung my suit jacket over a kitchen chair and continued to read. I was conscious of being tired and hungry but the stark lines of advice, echoing down from two and a half millennia, were beginning to chime with the details of my own dilemma. It was astonishing, although each topic discussed was clearly military in nature, the concepts and principles behind the advice had a universal truth. I dug out my Montblanc pen and Moleskine pad and started making notes. Soon the page was covered with writing, linked by big looping arrows. In the ancient wisdom I found strategies and tactics that I could use at the EGM. Now I had a battle plan.

shivering with fright
I step into the new year
no turning back now

Nawarra

When the music began on that majmical night
And she swankled down through us and onto the
stage
A flankulous pack of poliferous modents
Comploded before us - a chest full of treasure
With a jazzle of spangulant zhing and a half
And a good splosh of terral thrown in for good
measure

She was dressed head to toe in the whitest of white
With a floppett entirely intensical blue
A lady of epic comportions and clearly
Knew quite what to do with them and she intended
To swaggle her proppage and all of her fou-fou
And roop us complimely before she was
ended

Well she sprankled her floppett so spately and light
That we found we were all on the edge of our seats
And she waggled her poke in a schoolmarmish way
Her crowler she whippled to the shape of a crown
Just like she was making blancmange.
We were roopered!
"Aiwa", we all said as she brought the house down

Bernadette Smoczynska

Resolution - Reverend Scrivener

Graham Horder

Reverend Scrivener awoke early again, following a restless night. He walked over to the window, drew back the curtains, and saw that the sun had barely begun to rise over Exmoor. There was just a hint of glow creeping over the brow of the green hills, across the valley from the Rectory. It was a very large home, and he often felt the loneliness of his solitary life magnified by the tall walls and long corridors of this grand manse home.

"Still," he thought, "I shall not be lonely for long today." Friday was always a busy day, but today the wall calendar, affixed to his study wall, above his grand oak writing desk, looked crammed full to bursting. He paused to consider the coming day.

He had worked late into the night preparing his sermon for the eight thirty morning service, which began his Friday work day, so he knew that was first. At ten o'clock he had a meeting with a young couple planning to marry in the autumn. He always enjoyed seeing young love blossom, and cherished his role in developing the basis for a sound, Christian marriage. Today, though, this would be tinged with a hint of regret at his own love, lost.

Midday would see service at the opposite end of the spectrum, as it was the funeral of old Tom Benson from Upper Challacombe Farm. Tom's final years had been spent as a virtual recluse, and despite the Reverend's best efforts, no family had been located. It promised to be a dour and sad end to a lonely life.

The afternoon held a long band practice, where Reverend Scrivener led the group on his trombone. The twelve piece group were due to give a performance at the following day's Cottage Garden Society Exhibition in Ilfracombe , so everything had to be *just so* by then, he thought.

This particular Friday evening held the dubious pleasure of the Annual General Meeting of the local Rechabite Branch. 'Those people,' he thought, 'are *perhaps the only people in North Devon more puritanical even than myself!'* This at least made him chuckle, as his mind turned to what he should say in his address to these most religious of folk.

But for now he had his time alone with God. He said brief morning prayers, before fixing himself a large bowl of steaming, creamy porridge. This always set him up well for his long morning *prayer walk.*
He strolled along the hilltops overlooking the village. Here he felt close to his God and close to his beloved village.

This morning was different from most, as he was troubled in spirit by the new arrival of Sergeant Harry Cooke, after several years away on active service in India. His prayers were more distracted than usual, as he asked for God's blessings upon Combe Martin and her people, and on the coming days of harvest.

He walked down to the seafront, and then back up the long High street to the Church. He liked to spend time in the old building after his walk, to meditate and pray within the *holy walls* as he called them. At eight it was usually still a quiet time of the day, and he sat at the front and bowed his head. No sooner had he began his prayers than he heard the sanctuary ring turn and the door timidly open. He looked up and saw Amelia Hayden-Jones, an irregular church goer, but someone he had known since christening her almost forty years previously.

Amelia came tentatively down the west aisle towards Reverend Scrivener, and he could tell as she got closer that she had been crying. He stood up from his pew and walked up the aisle to meet her.

"My child, what is it that troubles you at this hour?" he asked. Her tears again began to flow as she poured out her anguish to him.

Ben Richards's fields were quite steep
and all of his girlfriends were sheep
he'd hop into bed
with his cap on his head
and count 'em 'til he went to sleep.

Letter From Millie

*Adapted by Chris Batstone from a cruder,
ruder version written by Basil Smale.*

dear eddie

yesterday i dug with my friend sybil who is super good at digging and is a collie a really good hole but something made the basil person shouty it could not have been us as we did not dig in the flowers which made the anita person basil's friend shouty we dug in the middle of the lawn which he complains about all the time when he makes the grass short what is a bear trap then they watched something called lassie about a dog that came home but we just slept they thought it was nice then barney came he has to travel on the seat in the big car he is not allowed to ride in the fun box of good smells with the muddy boots and old wax jacket that smells of cows like i am he is a boy so we chased up the garden and but he kept stopping to sniff at everything and he can wee so much he is super good at weeing he is a boy he likes balls and can make them squeak and he licked the cat sick on the carpet and then he found food on the table that he ate even though it was metal and shiny and did not look like our food and it made him do super big farts and then another human appears very shouty and barney runs up the garden and hides in a shrub and sybil does a wee because it is like when we rolled in the super whiffy fox shit and there is more shouting so we are shut away the basil person sneaked in with a bonio but the anita person caught him and now he's in the dog house too.

i miss licking your face

millie

Ghostly Lament

Of my love it seems, there can be no ending
Though ending I had thought, was upon me now
My feeling and passion remain, unbending
But what good can this be, to me, anyhow
Oh how I ache for the love we once shared
As I walk in the haze of summer, now lost
As I pause to gaze at your form to me bared
The bright sunshine now turned, embittered to
frost
I know that you have the same love for me still
And this burns more than words could ever give
tell
To follow, as you wander, as you weep and mill
Gives me cause to ponder, to long even for hell

    If eternity were, to be such as this,
    I would give it all up for just one more kiss

Graham Horder

Tiger

Tiger's soul sounds forth
To all who care to listen
Jungle master speaks

Eyes burning brightly
Big cat watches steadily
I honour you too

Momentarily
Eyes blink, jaw yawns wide open
Pondering next move

Back arched, paws extend
leaning back ready to spring
Forward to catch prey

Powerful leaping
Paw swipes sideways through the air
Prey lies on the ground

Chomping jaws tearing
Snapping teeth ripping carcass
Lips licked, meal complete.

Helen Weaver-Hills

Bluehaven Revisited

Early morning -
The village awakes
To the throbbing
Of the 7.25 bus.
Sleepy passengers
Yawn and stretch
Whilst the crows
Chatter on chimney pots.

It's a time of stillness
Punctuated by solitary figures
And speeding cars and vans
Hurrying to jobs in the town
Eager to see the day through.
Whereas I sit here, smugly,
Coffee in hand, with dogs prowling
High on retirement bliss.

There were times,
I have to admit,
When all was not so cosy
In that haven of blue.
Dark clouds passed overhead,
Storms raged within,
And I was left wondering -
What and why and when?

I'm back in my old house
Looking forward to this one
My heart warms at the prospect.
Life feels good again!
Thank God it took so little
To change the scene and mood
The sun came out - as now -
Greys have turned to gold and blue . . .

Don Hills

The Storm

Lightning flashes. Thunder rumbles.
Hailstones clatter on the pavements
the wind roars and fences rattle
trees and branches bend and sway
air rushes through every crevice
draughts shriek at windows and doors
raindrops pummel the window pane
tyres slush through puddles.

Sunbeams appear - birds twitter
wafts of air move gently around.
Silence descends once more.

Helen Weaver-Hills

A Day to Remember

Olive Gallagher

I had walked up West Challacombe Lane and the little rocky footpath, negotiating the minute stream of water that seemed to flow incessantly to reach the top of Wild Pear cliff. It was a quiet afternoon in November of last year, and as I stood gazing over the cold grey sea of the Bristol Channel, a small ship came into view. A chill went down my spine as I had a moment of déjà vu, recalling a similar scene on a chilly autumn day, so like this, on another part of the English coast, so long ago.

It was a late November day in 1939. I had called good-bye to my kind landlady in the big house in Hall Lane, Walton-on-the-Naze, and walked down the little footpath by the side of the garden to call for my friend, Mary. She was billeted with the coastguard's family in their bungalow at the rear of the coastguard station, which was perched a short distance back from the little crumbling cliff. Mary and I were probably the only two evacuees from our school that went home for lunch, as most of the girls were provided with sandwiches and stayed in our temporary classroom for the day.

I reached the cliff top some twenty feet above the long sandy beach and paused to take in the view – so different from the London streets where I had been brought up. The sky was almost colourless, just a pale, cold grey and the sea still and steely, dead looking, without apparent movement; sullen and silent; no surf and no waves to break the monotony.

At least it didn't look as terrifying as it had a few weeks ago in the October gales. One morning we had seen two enormous mines that had been washed up on the beach. They were great spherical objects, as tall as me, and covered in huge spikes that I knew would detonate on impact with the hull of a passing ship. We saw the minesweepers out every day, and often heard the explosion from the captured mines that had been taken out to the marshes for disposal.

Mary came down the path from the bungalow and we called into the lookout station to say cheerio to her host. He was a friendly man and we chatted with Uncle, as he liked to be known to the evacuees, for a minute. I looked out to sea from my vantage point and through the long sloping window could see a huge ship appearing from southwards, just passing Walton Pier. She wasn't far out to sea; not more than half a mile and was moving fast.

"Making for Harwich!" said Uncle and handed me his binoculars to have a better view. I saw her clearly, speeding along, and read 'TERUKUNI MARU' on her side with oriental characters underneath. She was magnificent. There was a great red circle proudly emblazoned on her bows.

"Japanese!" said Uncle. "One of their big liners, you know – like our *Queen Mary*." Japan, of course, was still neutral at the time. I could see Harwich quite clearly through the binoculars, a few miles north of us. There were fifteen barrage balloons floating above it, for protection from enemy aircraft. I glanced back at the approaching liner, which was almost level with us now.

Suddenly, there was a dense black cloud of oily smoke and orange flame erupting from the stern.

"She's struck a mine!" I screamed, my hands shaking as I handed the binoculars back to the coastguard. Then we heard the deafening roar of the explosion.

I could only stand and watch in horror. There was nothing I could do to help. The liner was shaking violently from side to side, as if it were a toy. I thought the mine must have struck the engine room. She came to a sudden halt and was already sinking stern first.

Uncle seemed oblivious to our presence. He was speaking into his radio. He was speaking on the phone. He was alerting every authority necessary.

Within a couple of minutes we could see men racing along the pier. The lifeboat was launched swiftly down the ramp at the pier's end. Men were running towards the beach. Every little rowing boat or motor boat available was heading out towards the stricken vessel. I saw the butcher, still in his striped apron, running for his boat further down towards the town.

A whole fleet of tiny craft appeared near the bow of the Terukuni Maru. They were shallow little boats with little curved white sails with the Rising Sun in the centre of them. They looked like miniature Viking ships making for the shore.

The liner was settling swiftly by her stern in the cold grey North Sea. It was forty-five minutes before the sea finally washed over her decks and claimed her. Great circles of water spread outwards as she disappeared from sight. I thought of all the people who may have perished in the sea or been killed by the initial explosion and I felt so useless because I was unable to help.

...

When it was over Mary and I solemnly said good-bye to Uncle. He looked as stunned and shocked as we must have done. We made our way back to our temporary school in the dining room of the pink-washed Raneleigh Hotel opposite the pier. Miss Goble and Mrs Page, our teachers, looked astounded as we entered.

"Why are you so late?" they demanded. They looked at us, in amazement, as I told them the events of the afternoon. Everyone in our school had been completely unaware of the drama occurring so close by. I was conscious of forty gaping mouths and pairs of eyes staring in horror as my story unfolded. Mary quietly sobbed.

At the end of my narration, Miss Goble gently told Mary to sit down, but she told me to write an essay about the scene I had just witnessed for homework that evening.

It is still as fresh in my mind now as it was then, although it was with great relief I learned many years later that the Terukuni Maru was not carrying many passengers and they had all survived the disaster.

...

I pulled myself out of my reverie. I was not staring at the North Sea but at the Bristol Channel in peacetime England. I am no longer a child. My stiff knees told me that I am an elderly lady who ought to be making her way down the steep hillside to Combe Martin before the daylight was gone.

For My Grandson

After Looking Through Some Old Photos

Have I really lived my life all these years -
The ups and downs, the ins and outs of time,
A time with many joys and many tears -
A dream world where those ghosts and
                                    shadows mime?
Yes, it's true - these photos show me at two
Facing the world in short pants, with a look
That seems to say -"I'm me, but who are you?"
A question I ask as I write my book.
I tried so hard to make my way through pain,
Finding refuge in adventurous schemes
To calm the restless sea - but all in vain,
These photos cannot lie, nor can the dreams.
Pictures mingle with words in my story,
Plenty of power, but not much glory!

Don Hills

The chef at the Royal Marine
serves a carvery fit for the Queen
a good choice of meat
all the veg you can eat
and the puffiest Yorkshires you've seen!

The Propeller

The
propeller starts
to rotate gradually
picking up speed
as it begins to
churn up
the
water   beneath
the surface   moving the
boat along as   life-forms have
their peaceful   existence below
the waves   interrupted

Helen Weaver-Hills

The Gift Of Chocolate Ganache To Prince Harry

Chris Batstone

When my wife and I were running a dairy, our proudest memory was winning two Taste of the West awards with our fresh chocolate sauce. The award ceremony was hosted by Prince Charles at his Highgrove home and Rick Stein was the guest speaker. He was accompanied by Chalky, his irascible Jack Russell terrier.

Originally we developed the sauce for Green and Blacks. The contract was dropped after they were sold to Cadburys, so we continued to develop it for our own dairy. We made the sauce the same way as a ganache, by mixing fresh organic cream with a high quality couveture chocolate.

Before the ceremony, we went on a tour of the Highgrove gardens, which gave us a very revealing insight into the character of Prince Charles. We felt a strong hint that he might have been more at home in an earlier, more romantic age. He delights in elaborate topiary and his gardens are full of hedges and bushes, cut into astonishingly ornate baroque shapes. These gardens are also the repository for his eclectic collection of large statuary, much of which is presented to him in his Royal duties. The most intriguing feature is the hidden arbours within shaded glades, concealed around the grounds. We were told that the Prince built them to provide peace and quiet, a refuge from his pressured public life. The stumpery, for example, is constructed entirely from huge, uprooted tree stumps piled up to form a semi-circle. Now beginning to decay, these are covered in moss and lichens so that their tangled roots, interspersed with dark ferns, create an eerie, melancholic atmosphere.

The ceremony itself brought more surprises. The Prince gave a very well informed and technical talk about sustainable agriculture. As the morning progressed, it became apparent that the guests were significantly outnumbered by the Prince's aides. After the awards were presented, we were told that the Prince would like to meet us informally. This was carefully choreographed; we were each given a precise spot in which to stand, so that the Prince could have the impression of meeting us by chance as he progressed around his guests. When I shook his hand I was surprised to feel that it was rough and calloused, just like a farmer's.

After we had been "randomly" presented, an aide asked if we had any spare chocolate sauce for Prince Harry's birthday party the next day. Fortunately, we had brought a lot of samples in a large cold box. With great excitement we went back to our car and fetched them all to give to the young Prince. We had visions of an excellent day being crowned with the accolade "*By Royal Appointment*".

Over the next few weeks we phoned Prince Charles' office to find out if our chocolate sauce had been a success, but there was no response and we never found out whether it had been enjoyed.

A year later we finally got a sense of how well it had been received; Duchy Originals launched their own chocolate ganache sauce. Perhaps imitation is the sincerest form of flattery?

Intranet

Don Hills

Glen Monks was a model employee.

At his interview, he answered correctly about the company's intranet policies. He'd mugged up on many of these, learned all the jargon: 'functional plans', 'information architecture', 'implementation schedules' and the 'phase-out of existing systems'. He quickly learned, once in post, about how to define and implement the security of their intranet structure; how to ensure it worked within legal boundaries and how to protect against viral sabotage. And, glory be, he could even offer an educated opinion on whether the input of new data and the updating of existing data should be centrally controlled. In short, he really was the model employee.

But, beating beneath that institutional breast was another beast, something wild and untamed. At weekends he was much taken with prancing around his flat totally naked, with curtains closed, to the accompaniment of wild, primitive music. He didn't dare turn the music up too loud. Nor could he dress, when it came to going out, in anything other than conventional suits, ties and shirts. With such a split in his life, he could see himself rapidly heading in a schizophrenic direction, but what could he do about it?

Now, Glen had heard about psychotherapy and knew from tentative enquiries that he could just about afford it, but something stopped him from taking that route. After all, he reasoned, what was wrong with leading this so-called double life? He wasn't doing anyone any harm and maybe being a company man from Monday to Friday and a wild man during the weekend was perfectly acceptable.

This was until Glenys entered his life.

He met her at an office party, where they laughed about the similarity of their Christian names. Almost without thinking, he asked her for a date for the following night. This happened to be a Thursday – only one day from his next *liberated* weekend. How on earth would he handle a date which bristled with potential difficulty, not to say heartache? Sure enough, the first topic at the meeting was the coming weekend:

"So tell me, what do you get up to, Glen … something a bit wild and whacky?"

Glen was taken aback. Did she know something about him that he had thought was safely captured in a box labelled *private*? He noticed that she smiled during this first question, so he smiled back and ventured, "Well, as a matter of fact, you're not miles off the mark. Sometimes I feel a bit trapped inside our company's walls. I need to break out a bit. How about you?"

"Ditto, ditto," said Glenys, with a broad, encouraging grin. "It's all that 'intranet-speak' that gets to me. Why can't we just use plain language?"

"Careful!" said Glen, warming to the exchange with rising confidence. "You're speaking to the man who <u>invented</u> some of it!"

"Aha, so it's you I have to thank for my sleepless nights, worrying about completing my performance targets."

"I plead guilty. What shall my punishment be?" he asked hopefully.

"A weekend of riotous living, which has to include me!"

Glen could hardly believe what he was hearing – a fellow liberationist!

"Your wish is granted, madam. How about tomorrow night at the Tropicana? I hear it's unbelievable."

"You couldn't have chosen better, Glen.   But make sure you dress the part.   I certainly will!"

-◆-

Melodeon

Squeeze boxes
A simple sailor can
play a jig
quickly pick out a tune
rough fingers
press easy keys Pleasant
melodies
from salt sea calloused
bellows blow
out and in and out

Chris Batstone

Epiphany

~Moonlight
Splintering the waves
Into chuckling gemstones;
Muddy shadows on the riverbank
Whistling round the holt;

~Otter and cub
Entwined
Like a wildlife Christmas card
Without the virginity;
Watery slides
Without the snow;
Fresh fish uncooked
Posted between the roots
Of an undecorated tree.

~Man
Hunting for sport
Taming shadows,
Fishing the moonlight out of the river,
Dancing unnecessary death;

~Fear
Five senses poor
Sports no peace or goodwill,
Yet keep otters alert for survival,
The heartbeat of labour;

~Mother and Cub
Relax in warm fur,
Their holt is dark, clean and dry.
The life of the river greens the air
Bubbles and echoes
The hounds have spared bitch and cub
This time
But the father has made
The ultimate sacrifice
Further upstream;
The red of birth and death
Staining the evergreen.

~Full moon
Splintering the wintry branches
Carves their shadows
Into wombs of spring buds
And next year's cubs.

Helen Robinson

blackbird sits on branch
calling sweetly to his mate
nesting time is here

My Twelfth Birthday

Helen Weaver-Hills

It's the nineteenth of May 1961. My brother Graham - six years my junior - and I are sitting on suitcases on the edge of the long, deserted dock alongside the *Diana* - a cargo ship in which we had just arrived at Naples. Our parents were busy with the Italian gentleman from the Automobile Association, whom they had arranged to meet on our arrival. He was standing by a little black Austin 30, scratching his head and jabbering away in Italian. The only phrase we could catch hold of was the repeated "*Mamma mia! Mamma mia!*" as he waved his hands in the air.

The car was pushed the length of the dock as we watched our parents become smaller and smaller in the distance. There was no-one around. Just the family and this man whose job it was to get us mobile. A jeep was commandeered and persuaded to tow the little car the length of the dock, but to no avail. There was a distinct lack of life in her engine. She wasn't going anywhere in a hurry. The concern on the adults' faces was increasingly obvious. We had a long journey ahead of us - several thousand miles to be more precise!

We had brought the car with us, in the ship's hold, all the way from East Africa. Our momentous journey had started in Kampala, where we had lived for the previous three years. My father was on six months leave from work and had made arrangements for us to travel by ship and car all the way to Thurso, at the tip of Scotland, to visit his family; we would then return, by similar means of transport, to begin another three-year term in East Africa.

Our journey had begun with a lengthy drive across Uganda and Kenya, following the long, straight, grey ribbon that stretched behind and ahead interminably, as we made for the coast and Mombasa, where we were to board the ship three days and one thousand and five hundred miles later. Along the way, we passed the point where there is a huge sign stating that we had reached the Equator. My mother duly stopped the little, cramped vehicle so we could stretch our legs and take photos marking the occasion. The car was laden down with all our camping gear on the roof rack - there were no plans for our staying in hotels as we made this memorable journey, apart from Rome - when we got there! The tiny boot was just big enough to hold four small suitcases - each measuring eighteen by thirteen by four inches and containing all the personal belongings we needed for six months.

"When are we going to get there?" was a constant accompaniment from the young passenger sitting beside me on the back seat. No personal CD players or hand-held Game Boys in those days. There were so few vehicles we couldn't even play 'spot the number plate'. We had to amuse ourselves. The scenery - for the most part huge expanses of dried, dusty earth, sprinkled with small thorn trees, bejewelled with the hanging nests of weaver birds - sped by on both sides for mile after mile. Most of the time we were the only visible vehicle on the road, passing the occasional bicycle, and here and there a giraffe or buffalo, which could be spotted in the distance.

After an exasperating and increasingly worrying couple of hours, during which everything possible had been fiddled with in the engine, my mother gently said "Have we put any petrol in the car?" A quick bump-start soon got us on our way together with the Italian, who insisted on being given a lift back to his office. My father, who was driving, was reluctant to stop the car after such a short distance. It came as no surprise when the car stalled and wouldn't start again! We were half way up a very steep hill in Naples, which was the main thoroughfare in and out of the city. No-one was taking any notice of us and it was left to my poor mother to push the car on her own, as we turned to face back down the hill so we could re-start the engine. Graham and I were leaning over the back seat, watching as the car jerked into life and we took off down the road to the clamour of horns, leaving my mother stranded amongst the traffic as she tottered on high heels, trying to run after us.

"Mummy's getting left behind!" we shouted at Dad, who eventually managed, against the angry tooting, to pull in just long enough for her to jump into the front seat before we were swept away in the onslaught of unforgiving drivers.

Heartbreak

Snow falling softly
Covering the fields and roads
Obscuring vision

Just like the blossom
That fell on our wedding day
Just a few months away

No birds fly today.
Sad and silent they're perching
Huddled in hedgerows

The snow is drifting
Covering sheep in the fields
Freezing and killing

Soft and white it looks
As white as my wedding gown
As soft as my veil

But now you have gone
My heart's in an icy grip
Freezing and breaking

Icicles forming
Freezing my heart and being
So deep within me

The ice on the lake
Like your heart, is treacherous
Would give way and drown

When the south wind blows
Ice will melt on the river
But will my heart thaw?

Snow will be melting
Green shoots break through the moist earth
Flowers bloom again

On these frozen boughs
New buds will soon be forming
Blossom break anew

But will my heart heal?
Will the green fields and flowers
Bring me joy again?

Olive Gallagher

Love Poem

It's true that I love all creatures great and small -
So what makes our love special?
Perhaps when light catches your smile
And time stands still.

But I love you too when pain prevents the smile;
When anxious thoughts invade your soul,
And I am drawn to your distress -
Like a moth to the flame.

I cannot analyse these moments of love -
They are simply part of my life.
Without them I would be swept up
In a sea of trouble.

Don Hills

From Combe Martin to the Gambia

Graham Horder

Banjul Airport. Two p.m. The heat hits us like a sledgehammer in the chest as we disembark down the steps and onto the runway, through passport control and on to the scrum which is baggage reclaim. Here, however, the game is complicated by a plethora of hovering and swooping trolley vultures, who will have your bags onto their purloined trolley, and headed out the door, before you realise the bag is gone! "Be polite but firm," we were told in advance, and now the challenge of walking that knife-edge comes into sharp focus. Welcome to Africa!

Having negotiated the pleasantries of the airport, we are herded onto the obligatory transfer bus. As soon as we are on the road, we are confronted by an unusual traffic jam. A large herd of long-horned cattle is being driven along the main carriageway by two hapless herd boys! Welcome to the Gambia!

After thirty hours on the go, we are relieved to arrive at our hotel. We are promptly assigned a room, and eagerly head off with the bag boy. Oh, boy! This room has seen better days; probably just after World War II. But it has a certain homeliness to it if you ignore the damp and decay. We unpack and contemplate the coming adventure.

Five p.m. really is too early to hit the bed trail, much as we are tempted, so we decide to have an exploration of our new environs. But, what's this? The room key will not come out of the door. Trapped! We summon help from our neighbour, and puzzle as to what exactly is going on in their room. There is a guy on the balcony with a toilet pan and some welding equipment!

'Hmm, interesting. File that thought for later,' I conclude, as a handyman arrives to virtually deconstruct our door in order to set us free. An hour and a half later, we get to have that time of exploration and acclimatization. Seems the trolley vulture syndrome is endemic, as we are descended on time and time again, by what are quaintly termed 'busters'. This is going to be a bigger challenge than I had anticipated!

Back in the room (G13, by the way), and unbeknownst to us, trouble is brewing. We retire for the night. A cleverly purloined electric fan has kept us relatively cool, and we awake suitably refreshed, and ready for our first proper day.

But what is that odour? The room had not exactly smelled fresh yesterday, but can it really have been THIS bad? On stepping out of bed, the answer becomes painfully clear. You may recall a thought filed for later yesterday? Now is the time for that thought to come back and haunt me, as I slip and slide out of the door, almost breaking my back and both elbows simultaneously! Welcome to Badala Park Hotel!

Serekunda

Having dusted myself down (or rather, wrung myself out!) I report my woes to all and sundry, before heading in for breakfast. Breakfast will follow a familiar pattern for the next two weeks. Bread, spam and more spam. But occasionally they will throw in some eggs to vary it up a bit, and there will always be watermelon and banana to feast upon. Morning worship outside C block commences at seven forty-five a.m., so woe betide anyone who wanted a lie-in! We then outline our plans for the day at our inaugural group meeting. Most of the newbies (myself included) are to be whisked off to Serekunda Market for a "deep end" introduction to Gambian ways.

This begins with the requisite haggling session at the taxi rank, as the journey's price is tentatively negotiated downwards. We end up with two minibuses for five hundred dalasi (approximately eleven pounds and this is to include waiting for two hours and returning us to the hotel). A good deal, it seems.

Serekunda is the most densely populated area of The Gambia, and the market is alive with new sights, sounds, smells and sensations for Western senses. Hustle and bustle combines with heat and hassle to make it an unforgettable induction into Gambian life. Our eyes wonder at exactly how great and varied a load the local women can balance on their heads, as they walk serenely by. Even the young girls have large platters of chilled water in bags, balanced perfectly for the refreshment of stall-holders and customers alike. The incessant chatter of bargaining and hawkstering is punctuated for us by the call to prayer blaring out of the local mosque's tannoy system. The heat at times is simply overwhelming, and we take refuge in Lana's Bar to sample the local beer - Julbrew. At thirty dalasi (seventy pence) for an ice-cold bottle, I have never been so grateful for a thirst slaker! Curiously, we had been chatting to a local police officer on our journey, and he joins us for a drink and chat for half an hour! So laid back these Gambians!

We visit the local batik factory and market, where we haggle hard for a beautiful village scene on cotton cloth and also purchase some wood carvings and a large towel - after much to-ing and fro-ing. We pass by the Serekunda Kingdom Hall (these days the Jehovah Witnesses are everywhere) and head back towards our waiting taxis.

But no recollection of Serekunda Market would be complete without the most overpowering sensation of all. And that is the fish! A local staple food (or is it a delicacy?) appears to be smoked fish, cooked on the roadside and piled up at the front of stalls. This certainly is a treat for all the local flies, as they appear in superabundance all over them. Whilst undoubtedly contributing to the odour (or should I say stench), this fact does not seem to deter the Gambians, who consume vast quantities of this oceanic offering. The scent of a fish stall from a hundred yards will live long in the memory. But not as long as the full up-close-and-personal experience!

Patient Love

Patience and understanding
Warmth and compassion
All these emanate from you.

Generosity and kindness
Gentle and steadfast
This is the spirit of you.

A smile. A welcome.
An offer of help
Show just how much you care.

All these things
And so much more
Are why I really love you.

Helen Weaver-Hills

Bargleflump *Bár-gul–flump. Verb. Int.*

The process of waking for the first time after drinking heavily, attempting to stand only to collapse back onto the bed feeling sick and nauseous.

How do I feel this morning?
Darple; definitely a bit darpled.
Touch handsome, bristled gringrains,
rub rough prodders across tired lookers.
To see visions of golden glory,
But the mirror tells a stoomy story.
Evening spent foot-flatting, shoe
tapping, too much innocent home fizzbrew,
guzzled from greedgrand glasses.
Decorum departed as garpling started.
Lost my heart to the touch of Barbie slows,
Blond eyes, blue hair and a dinky-kiss nose.
Warm honeyskin scents in my head
entranced my dance into a lover's bed.

Chris Batstone

What Is My Favourite Place?

Bernadette Smoczynska

My favourite place has a rock and roll bed, a two-ring cooker with grill, a compact fridge and a sink with running cold water. It also has four wheels. My favourite place is a VW T4 Auto-sleeper Trident conversion with just enough room for me, 'e, and the dog, a camper-van with attitude and, of course, a name. Shirley is small but perfectly formed, with blue bedding and kettle to match her blue interior. She is a bijou, movable *pied-a-terre*, a room not with one view, but with as many as you desire. Wherever I am in Shirley, like a snail, I am home. I have everything I need: food, shelter and entertainment.

Shirley has reached the stage in her life where she is happy being herself, young enough to be fun, mature but not old. She can smile indulgently at the surfer-dude-cool vintage split-screens and has no aspirations to be a 'Winnebago'. Often the smallest outfit on site, she is unpretentious and quietly dignified alongside the larger and more sumptuous vans with their onboard showers, microwaves and satellite dishes. She knows she's just fine as she is and besides the advantage is hers, as very often she has the freedom to go places they don't. She's very happy for the push-bikes to come along for the ride and almost ecstatic when the kayaks join us. She would, of course, love to be able to roll out her awning a little more often, because that would mean good weather. The chance to try on her new 'camo-net' would be sheer bliss. In Shirley, life's an adventure! Even a biscuit and a 'cuppa' brewed in a car park is fun. We've spent many a happy weekend in far flung, exotic locations like Appledore, Abbotsham and Exford, and if we don't feel like travelling too far, the campsite up at West Seven Ash Farm has glorious views over Combe Martin Bay. She's taken me dancing on several occasions and once we went knitting. Mostly we just go to enjoy the great British outdoors, to see sunsets over the sea and sunrises over mountains, to wake beside a river or a lake. From my bed, I have watched lighthouses flashing their warnings to nocturnal seafarers, the comings and goings of boats in a marina and a naked man feeding pigs. We have had alpacas as neighbours and been bullied by swans. Thanks to the Caravan Club we have been privileged to stay in gardens, orchards and fields, in farmyards, boatyards, a timber yard and a skip yard, to experience a shower in a cowshed, a loo with no roof ... and plenty with no paper.

Laughter, music, and the tantalising aromas of cooking and campfires carried on soft evening breezes. Drifting off to sleep to the sound of the wind rustling through leaves or waves swooshing onto pebbles. Hearing raindrops on the roof whilst I'm cosy inside. Owls calling through the darkness and the midsummer song of a damn skylark at four o clock in the morning. New paths to explore, right from the door, in the early morning mists. Being completely alone and being with others.

All these things and more make Shirley my favourite place.

Restless Sea!

Oh! Restless sea, not content with your might
As the coast is savagely gnawed each day,
Until you've consumed all land in sight
And dominated the earth of man's stay,
Leaving him doomed to his wretched plight,
'Till all the continents are washed away;
Yet the coast, on grim resistance bent,
Challenges your energy, until it's spent.

On summer days on the golden strand,
Where children play and build in sand,
They all take risks, adventures seek,
So sure they're strong, yet find they're weak;
They stem the waves that lap the shore
Till, unsuspecting they play no more.
Your hidden greed reaches out from the deep
And takes them away while others weep.

The ships that ply across your face
With cargoes from the world around
Are taken from restless waves apace
And dashed against the rocky ground.
There below in the fathomless deep
To lie forever in silence ………… sleep.

Coast! Ships! Children ………… God sent!
Oh cruel sea! Are you still not content?

Ken Thomas

Resolution - Amelia

Teresa Curtis

An errant strawberry wobbled and escaped the confines of the pannier on Amelia's old black boneshaker, as she wearily dismounted and straightened her long dusty skirt. The sun beat mercilessly down from an azure blue sky, sending myriads of sparkling rays bouncing off the distant ocean. Disobedient tendrils of dark hair sprung from their tightly coiffed arrangement and her high-necked blouse was irritating her chin, but Amelia was in a happily expectant mood.

Two miles away, The Rooms in Ilfracombe was hosting the Cottage Garden Society Exhibition. She was taking her lovingly tended produce to be judged along with growers from the surrounding villages and was sublimely confident of triumph in her category.

Arriving an hour later at the exhibition, Amelia was pleased to see a happy throng of people in attendance. This was a popular occasion, competition was high. A motley band of musicians was enthusiastically drowning the chatter with lively music.

A greeting was softly whispered into her ear. Amelia swung round to face the one person she was hoping to avoid that day. Ray Williams, holding the hand of his daughter Lily, gazed at her with a soulful and reproachful stare. Amelia averted her eyes, muttered a polite reply and moved away. It had been months since their affair and she had promised the Reverend Scrivener on the day of her atonement to avoid all contact. She sighed. Ray was such a good dancer.

With a picture of the Reverend's stern frowning countenance in her mind, Amelia was startled to spot him amongst the musicians, earnestly playing a large trombone. How fitting, she thought naughtily ... after all, one needed a fair amount of huff and puff to prise notes from that particular instrument! Next to him swayed the violin player, Mr Jenkins, his nimble fingers extracting a most delightful dance melody that had her feet tapping. Amelia had only met Mr Jenkins once before and remembered being rather taken with his tall frame, distracted air and laconic smile. He nodded and winked at her. Amelia watched spellbound, enjoying the music, until it was time for the judging.

At three p.m., the judging for home grown produce began. There was much hilarity as Mr Creek arrived with his giant marrow. Every year, Mr Creek won first prize and every year he strutted around the village of Combe Martin with a self-satisfied smirk on his freckled face. This year however, a new contender had arrived. A dainty Mrs Cook was proudly displaying her exhibit, a marrow measuring at least a foot longer than Mr Creek's specimen. Mrs Cook's tall, strong son laughed in triumph as he proudly lifted the huge marrow for inspection. Amelia recognised him as Harry Cook, the soldier son home on leave from India. You could tell he was his mother's but as Amelia watched him frown in concentration she had a sudden memory of similarly tightly knitted stern brows but couldn't quite put her finger on who it reminded her of. Oh well, she thought, that conundrum could wait for another day. Amelia concentrated on the far more pleasing aspect of a brand new idea.

She would invite the Reverend Scrivener to tea on Saturday and ask him to bring delightful Mr Jenkins the violin player along. She may not win first prize for her strawberries, but a far more satisfying prize would be a potential partner for the forthcoming Carnival Dance, especially one with such an attractive and laconic smile.

A Wartime Romance

We met at harvest
By the fields of ripened crops
Hot September day

I was dust smothered
Chaff clinging to clothing
Your eyes clung to mine

Your platoon moved on
We could see your tanks churning
Black tracks on the hill

My eyes were straying
While we threshed the ripe barley
Thoughts stinging like husks

Each evening you came
And we talked in the hostel
Or walked down the lane

Talked beneath the tree
Heavy with ripe mulberries
That fell at our feet

Ordered to the front line
Young and foolish we married –
Twenty four hour licence

How soon you were gone
And how long the dark evenings
I wrote every day

Worked hard in the fields
Picking sprouts, dug the root crops
Heart in the front line

Twelve long months went by
Ploughing, seed time and harvest
'Til we met again.

Olive Gallagher

An Old Pugilists Tale

"When did I get so damnably old?"
the boxer sadly wondered
As he slouched soporifically in his favourite chair
And on his life, he pondered

"It seems like only last week" he mused
I would whip anyone who would dare
Hop over the ropes, and step into the ring,
At the Devon County Fair"

"Where did the time go?"
The years whizzed on by
Never slowing nor tarrying,
Just to let me "enjoy"
How I wish I could take back
Just one hour, or a day
But on time must rumble,
To the end of the fray

Once love had come his way, for a season,
Drifting in unexpectedly, as if on a breeze
But no sooner was it there, than it was gone
A joy too ephemeral, for such as him to seize

"Why did I ever let her go?"
he was often heard to mumble,
Foolish pride, and a restless heart,
are cause for many a stumble.
"I can see her now, pretty as a picture"
His heart with sorrow breaking
Too busy fighting the shadows though,
To have noticed the inner aching.

But now my whole life is stilled; it's too late,
For time marches on, never looks back nor waits
The final round beckons, ding ding, there's the bell
But for this old boxer, is it heaven, or hell?

Graham Horder

Truth

I sing the song the warriors sing
As they to battle go:
I need their strength. I need their truth
For soon I meet my foe.
For now I know what I must know,
To feel I've got some worth
What I can do to understand
Why I am here on this earth.

My battle's not with earthly might
Nor yet with heavenly hordes
It's with myself, both day and night,
With truth, and not with swords.
Don't need to know the ins and outs
The twists and turns of fate.
Don't need the rule book's heavy hand -
Just leave an open gate.

What I crave is life aflame,
The chance to do and dare,
To find my way through paths of doubt
And leave behind despair.
Sometimes I'll fail. Sometimes I'll win.
Sometimes I'll sweat and bleed -
But give me just one chance to show
Brave heart in word and deed

Don Hills

The Unwelcome Visitor

Olive Gallagher

It was a beautiful morning in late summer and the small group of boatmen chatted by their little craft on the beach.

"Not so good as when I were a lad," said Sam. "A few year' ago us could take out much larger boats, and come back fair laden with cod or mackerel. Now I make nearly as much money taking out holiday makers as I do for fish."

Some of the group agreed, but young Joe laughed. He remarked that Sam would make twice as much if he didn't miss the tide so often by being delayed in the bar of the local pub.

A trickle of hopeful looking holidaymakers was beginning to arrive. They selected their boat and paid over the few shillings required for a few hours sport out at sea. One discerning member of the arrivals spent several minutes inspecting the vessels before approaching Sam.

"You will take me along the coast?" he asked in a clipped and refined accent. "I would wish to be your only passenger, and I would pay you well."

Sam was surprised. "Sorry, sir," he replied, "I usually take out five or six people on a trip – expect to make twenty five shillings. One man isn't going to match that."

For an answer the stranger thrust two crisp green one pound notes into Sam's hand. "Now you will take me where I wish!" he said as he stepped into the little craft.

Sam made the boat ready and set off slowly past the harbour wall and into the bay. There was a good strong breeze and he hoped the waves wouldn't whip up too much in the three or four hours he intended to spend out on the water. He looked at his passenger, who seemed too smartly dressed for a day at sea. His jacket looked expensive and his trousers were of an unusual style, but Sam wasn't a sartorial expert. There was something odd about this fellow.

"You will go first westward along the coast," the passenger suddenly ordered. "I wish to see the small caves. Then we will look at the coast in the eastward direction."

Sam wasn't too happy about this. He was the captain of his little boat, and was not accustomed to being ordered where to go. Some passengers made requests, but didn't give orders!

"Do as I say!" the passenger said tersely. "And keep close to the shore here. I wish to take the photographs."

Sam felt less happy now. He wasn't going to keep that close to the rocky coastline. He watched as the chap took an expensive looking camera from the small case he carried. Most holiday makers were quite happy to look at the wonderful scenery and take the odd snap on their little Kodak's. He'd never seen anyone with a camera like this one before.

"Cut the motor! Hold the boat steady!" ordered the passenger.

Two hours later, after making very slow progress, almost to Ilfracombe, Sam had turned the boat and headed across the bay in an easterly direction as his passenger had requested. By now Sam had grown to thoroughly dislike the man. He couldn't stand his contemptuous manner and the icy look in his steely, blue eyes.

Soon they were passing the great cliff that stood eastwards of the bay, Sam cautiously avoiding the treacherous rocks of the headland. His little boat was close inshore now, and the tiny cascade of pure water that tumbled from the high cliff was visible. The passenger gave a shout of triumph, and went on taking photos before instructing Sam to return for home.

As they pulled away from the cliffs he leisurely packed away his camera. Sam rowed silently back towards the harbour.

After a while, to Sam's surprise, his passenger brought out what appeared to be a powerful looking torch. By this time they were approaching Wild Pear Beach, and although it was broad daylight Sam was shocked to see the brilliant flash of light that the torch emitted to beam across the sea. The bewildered boatman was even more surprised to see an answering flash about half a mile out. He could just make out a flat grey shape and the flash appeared to come from the small tower in the centre.

As his passenger continued to flash his torch, comprehension slowly dawned. A submarine! Suddenly it all made sense. This fellow was doing some sort of reconnaissance! "You're a spy!" he shouted. "A dirty rotten spy!"

The man turned and aimed a blow at Sam's head with the heavy torch and before Sam could recover his wits a revolver appeared in his opponent's hand. The next moment Sam was struggling in the water. He could just see his erstwhile passenger making off towards the submarine with his beloved boat. As he swam towards Wild Pear Beach, hampered by his wet clothes and a blinding headache, Sam wished he had never bothered to get out of bed that morning.

It seemed an age before he could drag himself up the beach towards the cliff, away from the incoming tide. Reaching safety he passed out from exhaustion. It was some hours later that he awoke to find the tide lapping at his feet and - miracle of miracles – his little boat washed up on the shore, gently rocking at the water's edge. Finding the energy, somehow he climbed aboard. The oars were in position and he pulled away around the cliff for home.

Where was the spy? Had he managed to reach the submarine? Had it really happened or was he having some awful dream? He felt in his pocket. There were the two pound notes –no longer crisp and new but soggy wet and almost unrecognisable. Sam scrunched them in his hand and threw them into the sea. He didn't want money from a spy!

Reaching the harbour he pulled his boat onto the hard-way and slowly made his way up Seaside for home – aware of the concerned looks from passers-by.

Outside the newsagents the placards were showing the latest incredible headlines. "PEACE IN OUR TIME" they proclaimed. Neville Chamberlain had returned from Munich in triumph – and had at least gained a little time to prepare for eventualities.

Sam was relieved. He wondered who would believe his story about a spy now.

A man swimming in Combe Martin Bay
lost his trunks in the water one day
he used an ice lolly
to hide his folly
which worked until it melted away.

The Autumn Gale

The afternoon seemed quiet and still
As I'd walked out to Hangman Hill,
But now the wind is rising fast
And angry clouds go scudding past.
The full moon rising in the sky –
Birds hasten home and so do I.

I hurry down and quickly reach
The curving cliffs by Wild Pear beach.
Out to sea the wild waves curling
On the rocks below are hurling.
I can hear the thunderous roar
Of waves below me on the shore.

I reach the shelter of the trees
With gasping breath and trembling knees.
The wind is shrieking all around
As I climb down the rocky ground
And reaching Cobblers Park at last
Feel the full fury of the blast.

The autumn tide has reached its height
And wildly in the fading light
The dashing, crashing billows rise
And send the spray into the skies.
I pray that safe all souls may be
Who have to spend this night at sea.

Olive Gallagher

The Little Pebble

Gentle waves washed over the tiny pebble
Back and forth it rocked
In the shadow of the sand-sculptured
prominence.
The evening sky darkened,
As clouds gathered on the horizon,
Droplets of rain began to fall,
Creating craters on the surface of the sea.

Waves began to form, growing in size,
The pebble was tossed from side to side
Picked up only to be dropped repeatedly.
At first the dance seemed fun
And full of glee, the pebble rejoiced until -
Into a crevice on a much larger rock,
The little pebble fell, stuck fast - unable to
move.

The rain stopped, the waves calmed
The night changed into day
Sun-warmed silence greeted the morn
Children came out to play and run
Some on their own and some with no-one.
Suddenly the sun disappeared and darkness
Descended once more.

'So soon?' thought the little pebble
'Am I never to see the sun again?'
A shout!
"Look what I've found, Dad! Can we get it
out?"
Two pairs of eyes appeared, blotting out the
sky
The pebble was pushed and poked

Until, at last, it was held in a tight grasp.
Slowly the world lit up - the sun appeared
Eyes smiled down with glee -
"What a beautiful stone!
Can I take it home with me?"

Helen Weaver-Hills

Fog

How short the daylight
On that late November day
Fog came so swiftly.

Out to the school gates
Clutching at my sister's hand
We could see nothing.

Heard adult voices
Parents calling children's names
My Dad's voice loudest.

He held us firmly
Guiding us through the dense fog
A torch beam useless.

Atmosphere so thick
Sulphurous, yellow and damp
Clinging to clothing.

We walked blind and scared
With no familiar landmarks
All sounds were muffled.

Millions of coal fires
Thousands of factories belching
Smoke from their chimneys.

Relying on Dad
To lead us through local streets.
Was blindness like this?

The fog is choking
Growing worse every minute
How far now to home?

Dad felt for lamp posts
Though no light was visible
They could still guide us.

"Thirty more, turn left
Fifteen more to cross the road
Twenty – then we're home!"

People are calling
"Which direction the High Street?"
Lost and bewildered.

At last we reach home
Haven of warmth and light
Once more I could see.

Eyes red rimmed and sore
Grime smothering our faces
We all smell of soot.

Olive Gallagher

Visiting Prague in February

Helen Weaver-Hills

The snow is falling softly. You are wearing a thick, warm coat, collar pulled up round your ears, eyes peering out of a balaclava, hands encased in fluffy mittens and feet protected with fur-lined boots. You venture forth into this other-worldly, snow-covered scene. As you climb the arduous hill, a doorway juts out onto the pavement, tempting you to step right in, as did 'Mozart' in *Amadeus*. However, as you pause on the threshold a large pavement board catches your attention, with phrases such as 'Hair of the dog' and 'Cats' whiskers' - names of some of the herbal teas served by this endearing café. You step inside. Pausing to adjust your eyes to the dim interior, your nostrils are immediately assailed by the aroma of coffee and the sight of exotic-looking gateaux on the counter at the end of this small intimate room. The walls are covered in memorabilia and the shelving holds rows of colourful, individually-sized teapots, each with a matching cup as the lid. Choosing a seat in the corner you breathe a sigh of relief to see the menu is available in English. The service is exemplary and you are soon ready to resume the labourious walk to reach the massive Prague Castle, with its three courtyards and bewildering accumulation of treasures, high above the town.

Looking down from above, you notice that your accommodation is nestled among many ancient buildings huddled together. This hotel in the Lesser Quarter is another smaller 'castle', with apartments instead of rooms, providing you with the facilities of a kitchen, dining area and lounge as well as the usual bedroom and bathroom. The only meal served by this hotel is breakfast - a sumptuous meal never to be forgotten, with everything imaginable being served - including Czech champagne, which delights the delicate palate at the start of the day. Perfect!

Exploring the city further, you cross the Charles Bridge, passing its sentry of thirty saints, into the Old Town. The buildings here are statuesque and comfortingly solid in their darkened, impermeable stone. By contrast, the shops at street level are rendered minuscule, like colourful 3D images backlit against the sombre walls. Occasionally blue displays of beautiful, iridescent Bohemian glassware shine forth to capture the eye. Walking through the narrow, cobbled lanes, you come across one of many large squares, surrounded on all sides by tall buildings. A group of people are all looking skyward and like yourself, wait patiently for the ornate clock, high above, to strike the hour. Across the way is a large church, beautifully decorated and filled with natural light. Resting awhile and wallowing in the warm colours of its interior, which envelope you like a cosy blanket, you silently offer thanks for this magnificent city and all its treasures.

A week is too short to discover this many-faceted jewel and you find yourself yearning to return again and again . . .

A Morning Walk

Bernadette Smoczynska

If you are lucky enough to live in North Devon, you don't have to go far for a good walk. One of my own favourites can be had right from my doorstep. Up the garden path, turn left and I am on the coast path very soon. Waking early this morning, I seized the chance to welcome the new day whilst the rest of the world was still sleeping. The dog leapt out of bed with enthusiasm and I think that if he could, he would have put on his own collar and lead.

Following the road around to the right, we leave the houses behind. We take a moment to lean on the simple wooden bridge and peer down into the stream before taking the track uphill to West Challacombe Manor. Once, we happened upon a fox standing in the middle of the road here. My goodness, we were all surprised to see each other! Today we are not so lucky.

Beyond the field gate outside the manor, sheep graze on silver, dew-jewelled fields and ethereal rivers of mist flow down the valleys in the morning sunlight. Rumour has it that the Manor is haunted. Whilst renovations were taking place, some workmen refused to work in certain parts of the building and at least one person I know is reluctant to be there after dark. We should be okay now though, because after a hard night's work all spectres ought to be tucked up in bed.

From the Manor, we clamber up a watery lane, over a stile and we are on the coast path. From here, when we have plenty of energy, we can turn right and head steeply up to Little Hangman. This morning however, our route is left, across the field where Ed can rummage happily through the bracken and I have the bench with a view to die for all to myself. The yellows, purples and greens on the hillsides rising from Wild Pear Beach are intense in the crisp, clean morning air. In spite of the early hour there are already one or two small boats bobbing about their business on sparkling, Mediterranean-blue seas. The coastline stretches past Watermouth Cove and Ilfracombe to Hartland and beyond. I wonder, as I always do when sitting on this bench, what insanity drives us to suffer the traumas of airport and motorway when we have all this right here.

Having sniffed and gazed our fill, the pair of us head homeward. Leaving the coast path behind us, we take the deep, green path to our left, strewn with pink campion, which drops steeply down the hillside and deposits us at last back at the bridge. Finally we retrace our steps to civilisation, coffee and toast.

The End of the Day

At the end of a day
Which was hijacked by grey
Five o' clock and it's night
And I click off the light
A rasp and a grate
As I slam shut the gate
The rattle of chain
Through the gate and my pain
The wind's moans and sighs
Carry animal cries
The wolf's lonely howl
Big cat's rumbling growl
An owl's sudden screech
From the whispering beech
And my primal despair
'Cos you're no longer there

Bernadette Smoczynska

Resolution -The Dance

Don Hills

The party at the Village Hall was in full swing. It had been a year of hard work for everyone, but the harvest was now safely gathered in and it was now time to let go of all cares. The atmosphere was one of joyful celebration.

A ragtime band from Ilfracombe had come over in one of Sam Colwill's coaches, pulled by one of his famous four-horse team of greys. The band was playing The Turkey Trot, and the Combe Martin locals were having a hilarious time sorting out the steps. Amelia, though, was an accomplished dancer, and the couples followed her lithe movements. She was dancing with Ray Williams, and he seemed inspired by her expertise. He didn't realise that Amelia was sparkling because the Reverend Scrivener had informed her that Mr Jenkins was on his way!

"Ooh, look at him!" cried Molly from the haberdashers. "Watch him, Amelia! You never know what he'll do next!" The crowd laughed, good-naturedly, and Ray winked at as many of the girls as his eye could catch. He'd had a few pints already, and his blood was up. Lily, his daughter, watched from the sidelines with some misgivings. She'd never seen her daddy like this before. As she looked around she noticed that nice soldier who had come to speak to her class, and, to her delight, he came over and sat by her, pint in hand.

"Can I get you a drink? Let me see - I think your name's Lily?"

"Oh, yes please, lemonade, please."

While he went to the bar, Lily began to get a feel of the pulse of the beat of the lively music, and soon her feet were tapping to the rhythm. A large figure glided past with a small slim lady in tow. It was none other than the Reverend Scrivener, and he was laughing good-naturedly. How different to his thunderous sermons on Sundays!

Sergeant Harry Cooke returned with her lemonade.

"Enjoying yourself, Lily? Like the music? How about we have a dance after you've finished your drink?"

Lily could hardly believe her ears, but, plucking up all of her courage, she nodded enthusiastically. When it came to the moment for dancing she very quickly lost all her inhibitions and just let herself be guided by Harry. He was a good teacher and to her great joy, smiled and congratulated her on her performance. She was in her own private heaven and found herself humming along with the tunes.

Her efforts had not been unnoticed by Ray and Amelia.

"You've got an amazing daughter there, Ray. You must be very proud."

"I've never seen her like this before. It's like I've got a new Lily. Her mother was an excellent dancer. She always wanted Lily to have dance lessons. I'll have to see about it."

At a pause in the dancing, tables were set out with giant hams, lobsters, mounds of strawberries, bowls of clotted cream. This was no time for delicate partaking – it was every man, woman, boy and girl for themselves! The air was filled with the pungent smell of smoked hams, local cider and the sound of excited banter. A heady mixture indeed!

When all was finished, off came the remnants of the sumptuous meal and the tables were put away. Then it was back to the dancing in earnest.

Carnival time in Combe Martin was a time for marking the end of another year of hard work in an era of pre-war optimism. What would lie ahead for the likes of Harry Cooke, Ray Williams and their respective families? Something surely not on the minds of the revellers as they wandered homewards later that evening... for now it was enough to enjoy the festivities and let tomorrow take care of itself.

A Sonnet

Hi mate! Happy birthday; fifty today.
Now you are too old to join a boy band,
wear skinny hipster jeans or a hoody,
display love bites, play rugby for England.
You can't say "cool beans", "Troll" or "L O L",
listen to dubstep, banging gangster rap,
enjoy "yooff" culture, have trainers that smell,
like Radio One, as Chris Moyles is crap.
You can have a subscription to Saga,
Dress badly, tuck your vest into your pants,
wear socks in sandals, drink ale not lager,
worry about pensions and investments.
But you are my friend and I am old too,
and won't be told what I can and can't do.

Chris Batstone

Talking with the Kidz

"Why don't you get a job and earn some dough"
"Sure ting, but laterz, cuz I gotta blow
Guh tuh guh, so see ya in a bizzle
Keep it real, fo' shizzle ma nizzle"

"Are you really going out dressed like that?"
"I can wear what I like, coz I am well phat"
"Well fat?" said I, "What?? Are you sure?"
"Err, yeah, it's not the 20th century no more"

"But really that skirt is awfully short –
Will you be warm enough?" was my retort.
"Totes, man, chillax, don't have an epi
I am not no baby, I don't need a nappy!"

"Chris, could you just turn the music down"
"Wot, I can't 'ear you, but don't have a meltdown!
Anyways we're going out now, for a while
"See you later masturbator" – "In a while, paedophile"

"What? What? What did you just say?"
"Oh shut up Dad, stop being such a gay!"
"Dat is sick blad, wick to the whack," said Dan
"You owned him then, U is well bad man!!"

"I give up" I exclaimed, as I storm to the kitchen
"Hey, look at my trainers Dad, ain't they bitchin'?"
"Not you as well!! I can't take any more!"
So I grab the rubbish and head out the door

Bins for this, bins for that, what a palaver
"Right, got it all sorted", but just when it's over
My son and his mate start to point and laugh
"Ha hah, look at your Dad, he's a Recyclo-path!!"

Graham Horder